The first day on the new Job...

"If you're quite finished lollygagging, officers?" The necromancer beckoned.

"Yes, Dermit?" asked my new partner. We walked over and circled the corpse. "What've you got?"

"Cause of death seems clear," said Cumberlan. He pointed to the man's neck. "Broken. Twice, actually."

"Uh, twice?" The Corporal shook his head and frowned. "How's it broken twice?"

"This is a bit strange in fact," said the necromancer. "The first time does not seem—"

"The first break didn't kill him," said Thief, cutting the old man off. "He lived though that, and the killer broke his neck again to finish him. The second time is lower, right?" The necromancer nodded as his eyebrows knit together. "Come on, Dire. We have somewhere to be."

I glanced at Hollin and widened my eyes. He gave me a little wave.

Half running, I headed off after my new partner; leaving the old one to stand vigil over my first homicide victim.

DIRE CALLS:
THE DIRE CRIMES SHORTS

THE PARTNERS

[ALL SIX WORKS BELOW IN ONE VOLUME]

PREDAWN RESCUE
DAY BREAKS
NOON HIGH
SUNSET RIDE
GLOAMING DEEPS
MIDNIGHT SORROWS

For a free electronic copy of this book,
send an email to
sales@oakenbrand.com
with a copy of your receipt.

Current List:
mathewreuther.com/works/

THE PARTNERS

DIRE CALLS SERIES 1

MATHEW REUTHER

Oakenbrand

OAKENBRAND.COM

Copyright © 2013 Mathew Reuther
Cover Design: Bridgette Reuther
Print Layout: Bridgette Reuther
Illustrations: Bridgette Reuther

Published by Oakenbrand Press
oakenbrand.com

First Print on Demand Edition: March 2013
ISBN: 9781939817037

Copies of this book are printed in the United States of America and the European Union as needed.

Dedicated to my firstborn son,

Ethan Gabriel,

who was taken from us far too soon.

Je papa houdt nog so erg veel van je, lieverd.

Rustig slaapen, m'n kleine engeltje.

TABLE OF CONTENTS:

PREDAWN RESCUE

DAY BREAKS

NOON HIGH

TABLE OF CONTENTS:

SUNSET RIDE

TABLE OF CONTENTS:

DEAD'S NIGHT

MIDNIGHT SORROWS

PREDAWN RESCUE

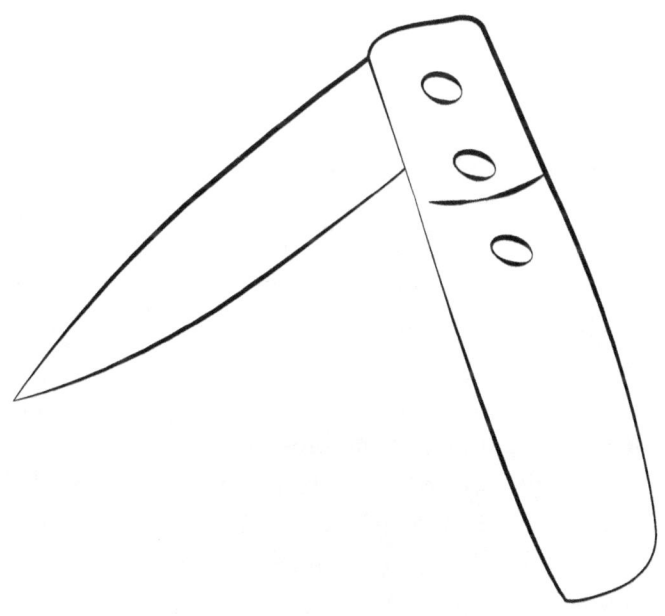

Driving rain which, two weeks back into civvie life, no longer seemed novel—even after the desert—had sent me scurrying into a filthy little dive before midnight. Cheap drinks and minimal questions had kept me in until closing time.

Beyond, even.

The limping dwarf behind the bar was a vet, mustered out years ago after some forgotten conflict in a thrice-damned backwater of the Thousand Kingdoms cost his leg. He proved lax about kicking someone like me out of the joint at closing.

Ex-soldiers have the Look. You can spot us a mile away. Hair, bearing, whatever. Time dulls such things, but I'd only recently been treated to having medals heaped upon my chest, then summarily drummed out. I was ramrod straight. Clean-cut.

When I saw the streets of New Dagonia again, the skies above the dingy buildings of the broken down ward weren't weeping, but light threatened to break through. I flexed a wrist, activating the chrono. 4:35AM hovered over my palm.

I yawned—producing a cloud smelling of alcohol and assorted nuts—and trudged down the empty street. Tipsy feet kicked the refuse scattered across the uneven stones of the sidewalk.

Somewhere around the corner—down half a block—waited my beat-up ride. The well-used Kandry Sparrow had lasted through university and three years of service, but the carriage was showing its two decades. Spending a year idle hadn't done the crystal drive any favors.

A cat yowled, standing my hair on end. I fumbled for keys before reaching the carry. As wards go, Black Spit isn't a place to linger. I pressed the key against the runes which pulsed and unlocked.

Cat sounds again; pained—or panicked.

I paused and strained, listening.

Another high cry. Not an animal; a woman's scream.

My heartbeat spiked; vision narrowed. The alcoholic haze receded as blood coursed. I pulled the door open and reached into the console.

The folding knife I retrieved wasn't a service-issue bayonet, but four inches of steel was a welcome companion. I opened the weapon and tucked it up my sleeve, inverted; like I'd drilled a hundred times—albeit with a wooden replica.

Training—and instinct—took hold. I flattened myself against the buildings and sidestepped towards an alley fifty feet ahead. A queer, naked sensation welled up as doubt struck me. I was a soldier without a long arm, or even a wand.

The woman's screams continued. The city-state might've been done with my services, but ignoring the officers' oath I'd sworn proved impossible.

I reached the corner and pressed back against it. Head in, survey; out again, assess.

Sixty feet away were five men, and at least three blades. One woman—probably a prostitute—half naked inside the bed of a lorry, screaming. A rail thin man pressed down on top of her, pants at his knees.

Breathe. Act.

I grabbed an empty bottle off the sidewalk and cradled its neck, then lurched into the alleyway. Softly lending a voice to a dirge from my childhood home, I wobbled towards the group; head down, eyes wary.

> *"The sweeping blast, the sky o'ercast,*
>   *The joyless winter day*
> *Let others fear, to me more dear*
>   *Than all the pride of May:"*

One of the men looked up. He grabbed the arm of his nearest companion. Both turned and walked towards me.

> *"The tempest's howl, it soothes my soul,*
>   *My griefs it seems to join;*
> *The leafless trees my fancy please,*
>   *Their fate resembles mine!"*

Yards separated us. I watched their long knives. "Hey!" said the fatter of the duo. "Turn your ass around and get lost, drunk." He punctuated the command with a flourish of his blade.

"Huh?" I reeled in mock shock; stumbled to the cobblestones.

The thickset man stepped in as I levered myself upright. "I said beat—"

A knee to his groin brought silence. The off-hand bottle throw went wide, but startled the second thug. I spun in and lashed out with my knife, cutting the back of his hand.

The greasy tough's eyes bugged out; he screamed and dropped his steel. That caught the attention of the others. The two holding the woman came at me with naked blades. They needed no urging; yet the fat man rolling on the ground managed a weak, "kill that bastard," before lapsing into mewling cries.

Seconds blurred. Drink slowed me, but I had better training. I parried a blade, dodged a board thrust at my face by the bleeding man, and managed to deliver a nasty slash to one of the newcomers' legs as he kicked at me.

I stepped inside the next swing of the plank and pinned the filthy punk's hand to it. The knife wrenched away as he fell, disarming me. I skipped backwards, avoiding the crazed arc of the last man's attack.

My feet fouled in refuse and I went down; impact rattling teeth. Shaken, I attempted to roll. A kick caught me in the gut, knocking the wind from me.

A hand grabbed my forehead; jerked backwards. Steel at my throat.

Bugger me.

A wand barked. Blood spattered against my scalp. The man collapsed, slamming my face into stone.

"...hear me?" asked a gruff voice.

I tried to sit, but a hand restrained me. I opened my eyes. My vision wavered, then cleared, revealing a grizzled, middle-aged man above me.

"Aye," I said.

"You're an idiot."

"What?" I tried moving. Pain shot through my head.

"Idiot. You." He gripped me under one arm and pulled. "Five armed men. You go in with this?" He handed over my blade, still covered in blood. "If they'd had wands—"

"She needed help."

He grunted. "You saved a detective, Mr.—"

"Lieuten—" I broke my lost rank off and felt a twinge. "Uh, former-Lieutenant Dire. Ex-NDA."

"Their loss." He waved towards the woman being walked away by a cop. "My squadmate."

"Didn't know."

"Thank you." He considered for a moment; cocked his head.

"Say, Dire, you ever consider joining the boys in gray?"

The answer which came out surprised me: "Aye. Just now."

DAY BREAKS

CHAPTER 1

I'm never late, so—of course—my first day as a detective started with the biggest traffic jam of the year. Hammersmith watchtower seemed an eternity away as I drummed four fingers on the wheel of my Sparrow. I had visions of walking into the bull pen only to be sent back out on patrol for tardiness.

Fantasizing about conjuring up a great bloody wind or summoning a huge elemental to sweep the carriages and lorries off the thrice-damned Archstone—as if I were a crazed wizard of yore—served as a distraction as I spent agonizing minutes creeping the carriage forward in the press.

And then—life being funny—dispatch broke through on my link. I was about to start the climb to the bridge deck, but the address drifting across the void required me to make hard course correction. I cut across to the exit and squeaked by the guard rail with an inch—if that—to spare. I trundled down the narrow shoulder, passing other angry commuters who shook fists and shot me dirty looks.

With no prospect of getting a carriage issued for at least a year I'd had the venerable Kandry worked over by a friend in the Archstone drive pool. Turned out to be a wise move.

A brake-check isn't my idea of a fun Monday, but I got to enjoy one nonetheless. A big, black monstrosity of a carriage—one of those that's half a lorry—lurched across the line to the shoulder, blocking me.

After I'd stressed my bubble—and worn some tyre off—I honked, waved, and got a rude gesture in return.

A low curse ended up muffled behind my grimace as I popped the door open. The carry wasn't going anywhere too quickly in this traffic, so I slow-walked towards the driver.

The polite tap on his window didn't seem to warrant any attention in the middle-aged orc's world. He made himself busy whistling and ignoring me. Honking started up behind us.

The traffic was thinning out ahead; space continued to open up. He didn't drive. I clenched my jaw.

Friday's bash had been worth a lot. I'd remember the party—what I could recall of it anyway—forever. But standing at a window being ignored sure made me miss the cherry I'd skipped picking up because we'd cut out early.

I slipped my case out of a pocket, flipped it open, and jammed the release. The brand new sigil flared to life, giving me a thrill as the gold blazed. I slammed it against the glass.

Mr. Smarty-orc's eyes widened as he caught sight of the symbol of my authority. His head jerked towards me and he lowered the window.

"Sorry, offi—"

"I have better things to do than cite you. Move your carry. Now." I turned on a heel and returned to the Sparrow. Seconds later I rolled past the orc and his toothy, sycophantic grin.

I ignored him.

The address was easy enough to reach using side streets, and I'd spent my first year on the Job patrolling Archstone. So just minutes after exiting the thoroughfare I arrived outside the warehouse. I pulled the carry off, parked it next to a marked unit, and hopped out into the brisk morning.

I grabbed my new fedora and coat off the seat and slipped them on as I headed inside. Habit dictated a wrist flick to do a chrono check, but I was interrupted before I could complete the ritual.

"Look who couldn't stay away."

I laughed. While my eyes hadn't adjusted to the dim interior, my ears were fine. "I missed you too much, Hollin."

My newly-ex-partner walked out of the depths of the building shaking his head. "Damn, Dire. What're the odds you'd get this call?"

"Well, assuming you have a body...."

He nodded. "We do indeed. Been here a while, too." I followed the Corporal into the warehouse. My vision adjusted as we made our way through tight, winding rows of mostly empty shelves. We emerged in a roughly square area at the rear. "Here's your vic, Detective."

A single metal chair sat in the approximate center of the area, decorated with the corpse of a human man. His skin was desiccated, giving him a shrunken, half-skeleton appearance.

"Where's Necro?" I asked, as I shrugged off my coat. The hot, dry air was stifling.

"Stuck in traffic, I suppose."

"You here alone? Can we find a way to shut off the heat?"

"Officer Colling is wandering around outside. Said he was looking for an override. Climate controls are jammed." He grinned. "I doubt he'll discover some secret switch though. I think Jame just doesn't like mummies."

I snorted. Jame Colling was my replacement. Not a bad cop, but Hollin would doubtless need to ride him hard after the kid's last partner. Sergeant Gamlin had suffered badly from short-timer's disease since before I was assigned to Archstone, and he'd finally retired three weeks ago.

"Sorry, Brees."

"Had to be someone, Griff."

"Aye." I turned back to the mummified corpse and took a walk around it. The man was dressed in neat clothing. His look was working class, but well-appointed and fashionable.

Exemplary taste hadn't saved him a beating though. I spotted a shattered cheek and jaw right off. As painful as that would have been, it was his hands that turned my stomach.

Every one of his fingers seemed like it'd been wrenched and broken. More than once for the longer digits. I shuddered.

"Grizzly, huh?"

"Someone worked him over bloody hard. And I think you're

right, he has been here a while."

"Maybe you can let a professional make that assessment?" I stood and nodded to the new arrival, an elderly necromancer carrying a field kit.

"Good morning." I extended a hand. "Detective Dire."

He mirrored the courtesy and gave a firm shake. "Cumberlan."

I stepped back, giving the Necro agent plenty of room to work. His job was to find out what killed the man.

Mine—find out who killed him.

Cumberlan got to work. He pulled a few solutions out of his kit and sprinkled drops across the corpse. Next came some powders. He'd begun to sort through a handful of different runes when my scrutiny was interrupted by a new arrival.

"Well if it isn't the idiot." My stomach flopped as I turned.

"Sir," I said, coming half to attention before I forced myself to relax.

"Shit, how long since you got out, kid?" The grizzled, graying man who'd asked me to join the force had an impossibly wide—and uncharacteristic—grin plastered across his face. He shook his head, sending his unruly blond mane flying, and chuckled.

"Long enough that I should bloody well know better."

"Good to see you, Dire."

"You too, Thief. Thank you."

"What for?"

"For getting me a slot."

Air rushed from the first class's pugilist's lips. "Your exam did that. The Captain was almost salivating on himself as he read them."

"Still, I owe you."

"My ass you do. Not after what you did."

Hollin coughed. "This would be the new partner then?"

"Detective Hargold Thief," said the bear of a man, extending his meaty paw. "You're Corporal Hollin. Brees, right? Heard good things, son."

The uniform returned the gesture. The two squeezed for a little bit longer than strictly necessary. When they let go Brees tucked the hand behind his back. "Griff's told me the story of how you suggested he join up."

"All he was missing was a sigil and a wand. Police spirit had a hold of him already."

I shrugged my shoulders and exhaled hard. "More like being mental after a year in the desert."

"Oh, yeah, that's some excuse." Hollin grinned. "Griff's still crazy, Detective."

"Lies."

"If you're quite finished lollygagging, officers?" The necromancer beckoned.

"Yes, Dermit?" asked my new partner. We walked over and circled the corpse. "What've you got?"

"Cause of death seems clear," said Cumberlan. He pointed to the man's neck. "Broken. Twice, actually."

"Uh, twice?" The Corporal shook his head and frowned. "How's it broken twice?"

"This is a bit strange in fact," said the necromancer. "The first time does not seem—"

"The first break didn't kill him," said Thief, cutting the old man off. "He lived though that, and the killer broke his neck again to finish him. The second time is lower, right?" The necromancer nodded as his eyebrows knit together. "Come on, Dire. We have somewhere to be."

I glanced at Hollin and widened my eyes. He gave me a little wave.

Half running, I headed off after my new partner; leaving the old one to stand vigil over my first homicide victim.

CHAPTER 2

Thief moved fast. Quick enough I needed to hustle to catch up, even being a few inches taller—and over two decades younger. We'd nearly cleared the building before I fell in beside him. "Where're we going?"

"Still driving the junker," he said, pointing at the Kandry.

"Aye." I nodded.

"My carry's this way, come on." He didn't slow up on our approach; he jerked the unit's door open, jumped in, and started the drive.

I'd barely gotten in when we peeled out and careened towards the street, narrowly missing a lorry. Hargold accelerated and began to weave through traffic before I'd even settled my bubble.

"The neck thing," Thief said as he slipped out ahead of a slow-moving carriage older than the Sparrow. "Not a new method of killing."

"So we have a suspect?"

"Yes and no. Lowlife enforcer who ran with a Kaid's Cross gang called the Tyrants of the New Order. Sent up to The Crag last year. Same hallmarks though."

"Sounds like we've got a problem. I'm assuming he's still there."

"Yeah. Goran's locked up all right."

"Copycat?" I asked.

"I don't know for sure. Not my collar, but I did hear a lot about the case. We're talking a very specific way to kill."

"Not to mention torture."

"The first break paralyzes."

"How can you torment someone after paralyzing them?"

"There you go, this is what's got me in a bad mood, newbie." He drummed four digits on the console. "Broken fingers, like the murder they nailed Goran on. Clear torture, right? Necro determined that the initial break, the one up top, is done in a way meant to leave the vic immobile, yet able to feel all kinds of sensations."

"How many people could possibly know about this method?"

"The question then is who'd the two-break killer teach his secret?"

On the off chance we'd missed the memo on an escape from Dunsmire Keep, I checked with dispatch. Confirmation came over the link within minutes. Goran was still rotting.

"So, we know our original murderer is locked up. Are we headed to rattle the Tyrants' cages?"

My question earned me an extended bout of laughter, followed by Thief going mute for the rest of the trip.

Which meant by the time we made it out of Archstone and into the less familiar—and definitely more seedy—environs of Kaid's Cross I got to enjoy the drive in silence. The streets of the ward were a bit nicer than those of Black Spit—where I'd first met Hargold—but it qualified as a downright inhospitable part of the city.

We passed several stripped carries on the back alleys Thief took to avoid the traffic. More than a few groups of idling citizens certainly not involved in anything close to legal business went by the wayside as well. But my partner's secret destination beckoned to him, and he studiously ignored the liri being handed over in exchange for illicit powders and crystals.

I kept reminding myself I'd given up the easy gold in the Substance Abuse Unit for a chance to put killers away. Drugs were a vice problem. Even the bodies which invariably dropped during drug transactions became a file to be shuffled around the Organized Crime Unit.

Unless, of course, the corpses belonged to important people. The gang boys handed the case up the chain to the real specialists in those instances. But these poor addicts—and even the kids who slung the junk because they were stuck with no other place to belong than their local tribe—weren't worth Homicide Unit's time.

Thief pulled the Hallowstone up beside an unexceptional rubbish bin in a nondescript alley and got out. I almost slipped on the dirty cobblestones as I stretched and performed a chrono check. 10:02AM. I recovered my coat and hat as Hargold popped the trunk.

He waved me over. "Take the rod."

I retrieved the weapon. Again, habit translated to action; I gave it a once over. Standard issue earth rods are good for close quarters battles. When you want to hit everyone in a general area, they're your best friend. They can also be tuned by narrowing the crystal's band; a tight setting makes it possible to drop a single person, so long as they're within about fifty yards.

The rod's charge read good. I turned; Hargold's expression was expectant. "What?"

He sighed. "Want a written invitation to make that thing scarce?"

I pulled my coat off and wrapped the rod in it. He grinned at me. "You need longer outerwear, newbie." He flapped the tails of his charcoal trench at me and sauntered out of the alleyway.

We made our way down the sidewalk two blocks before he stopped in front of a small entryway. "These guys don't like messing with cops. They're not fond of being messed with themselves. We should be fine, but remember: stay calm." I nodded, and he pulled the door open.

Loud, obnoxious music involving drums, fiddles, and flutes spilled out, filling the street. Thief ducked in; I had to half crouch to get through the portal after him.

Inside the establishment the ceiling wasn't quite tall enough for me to stand. I kept my knees bent, and folded myself over.

The smell was awful; whatever meals they served weren't meant for humans any more than the tiny stools which lined the bar and dotted the floor were.

The cacophonous noise stopped as all eyes turned to follow our progress. Thief kept walking towards the rear, so I trailed him. The Code read that the proprietors couldn't kick us out; they could refuse to serve us though, and dirty looks were still imminently legal.

Goblins aren't necessarily more dangerous than any other race. Sure, they engage in ritual cannibalism in some parts of the world, but most of them are work-a-day citizens, like anyone else.

As we wove our way towards a door—marked *private: get lost*—at the back, I got the distinct impression generalizations didn't apply to the occupants of this particular watering hole. Might have had something to do with the prevalence of knives, each just about the legal maximum four inches long, appearing as we passed tables full of patrons. In a goblin's hands blades that small give the illusion of being almost a foot in length.

"We're here to see your chief," said Hargold.

The goblin leaning up against the wall next to the door scratched his head. "Whatcha need?"

"That's his business," Thief feigned a yawn and didn't bother looking down at the guard.

"N' I say it's mine."

"Stop wasting our time. Get your boss," I said, slipping my unencumbered hand into a pocket.

All across the bar knives turned into wands in seconds. Half the patrons seemed to produce them from thin air. Fairly amazing considering your average wand is about as long as a goblin's entire arm.

Thief glanced over his shoulder and furled his brow. He turned slightly and waved a hand. "My friend just likes gum." He laughed. "You're all pretty jumpy. Acting like you've never seen a couple humans before."

"Humans don't come here."

"No?" Hargold's eyes went wide. "But you're so charming."

The door swung open. "Please join me, detectives," said the thick-armed goblin with a golden mane standing just inside the room beyond.

"Much obliged, Krane." Thief ducked and stepped through. I followed; giving the guard a wink for good measure. The growl my expression elicited clued me in to the fact that he didn't seem to like me much. I'm certain I didn't care.

CHAPTER 3

The small office we stepped into was cluttered with paper-work. Thief scooted the tiny chairs in front of the desk aside and pulled up a piece of floor. I knelt over his shoulder.

"So," said the goblin as he hopped into the comfortable chair situated behind the cluttered bureau, "I'm positive you didn't come to arrest me."

"Of course not," said my partner.

"I'm a law-abiding businessman."

"Oh, I'm terribly sure."

From a glance at some of the scribblings—all jotted down in Goblin, of course—I noted a whole lot of numbers next to a bundle of names. If Krane wasn't a backroom bookie, or possibly a loan shark, I wasn't a cop.

"Why is it that you're here, Hargold? Who's the new meat?"

"Detective Dire, meet Krane Branded."

"What? Leaving out my honorific?"

"Fine." Thief didn't put any extra weight on his words as he rendered a proper introduction. "Griffon, this is His Resplendent Majesty, Krane Branded, King of the Goblin Court."

I nodded my head. "Pleased to meet you."

"No manners on you cops," said Krane. Of course I knew the only thing he was King of was another of the city's multitude of gangs. All I could recall of the Goblin Court was that mainly they dealt in protection, book making, usury, and the occasional enforcement of their territory. Prostitution wasn't their thing. Not much market for peddlers of goblin ass.

"Now, now." Thief clicked his teeth. "You've got your subjects outside." He jabbed a meaty finger at the door. "But even in here you're still subject to our authority; and as I recall we're clear on that, you and me."

Krane turned a pale, sickly green. "Yes." He swallowed hard.

"Don't look so worried. I'm here to help you. You do me a good turn, and wonderful things happen."

"Everyone's happy?"

Thief nodded. "Well, maybe not everybody. But you and me? Yeah."

"What do you need?"

"Info—street level intel—on an enforcer who snaps bones."

"Lots of enforcers snap bones."

"He's not talking about goblins with hammers," I said, wanting to be a part of the conversation. I was the newbie cop swimming in deep waters, but I wanted to be noticed. "We want someone...big."

"My guys can—ah, goblins...." Krane sighed and looked away from me. "What are you wanting, Hargold? Be precise."

"I've got a body that seems like it's been worked over by your old friend Goran," said Thief. He cracked his knuckles, slow and deliberate.

"Goran's in the hole."

"I know, my squad put him there. You're welcome."

Krane tapped on the desk and rubbed the back of his bleached mane. "Listen, I heard a rumor—"

"Spill."

"It's just a rumor, understand?"

"Understood," said Hargold. "I want to hear for myself."

The goblin sighed. "You did not hear this shit from me. You were never here. Swear on Kestha's teats."

"I'll swear. Not on your earth mother's cans though."

"Fine."

"What, you actually want me to swear?" My partner shrugged. "Superstitious bastard, you are. I swear by, Jaros, may he strike me down for telling lies if I ever reveal my source."

The likelihood of Jaros—god of priggish fools by my reckoning—listening to a thing Hargold Thief had to swear was less than zero as far as I was concerned, but Krane took it.

"Goran's mother is back in town."

A low whistle escaped Thief's lips. "What do they call her again?"

"Crusher." The goblin shuddered.

"She's working with the Tyrants?" I asked.

"Probably half running them. Your gang boys grabbed their previous leader and two of his inner circle. They're awaiting trial so he's been out of it for months."

"How long has she been back?"

"Couple weeks. A month? Again, just what I hear."

Thief nodded. "Krane, you're too useful alive for me to leak, and Dire? Well, he's an idiot, but he's one of the smartest idiots I've met."

"Won't breathe a word," I said.

"Right, mind going out the back?" My partner growled—probably the lowest noise I'd ever heard a human make—at the suggestion, and Krane held up his hands. "Maybe nobody saw you come in, but why risk being seen on the way out?"

"Of course," I said, before my partner could answer.

"Excellent," said Krane. His face split into a toothy grin that reached almost to his pointed ears. "If you'll just wait one moment while I have a couple of my boys escort you. Wouldn't want you to get lost."

CHAPTER 4

Another half an hour of walking through sewage with a bag over the head seemed preferable to what I could sense brewing in Thief as Krane's Goblin Court flunkies set us loose. My partner's face was ruddy under his shaggy blond hair. Hair soaked with—well, probably not all sweat, unfortunately.

"So, what'd you learn?" asked Thief after the trio wandered off.

"Never trust someone who uses that much dye?" He grunted. No sign of the levity I'd hoped to inspire.

"Come on," he said, setting off out of the filthy vacant lot we'd been dumped in. "We need to figure out where we're at."

I followed as he walked to the nearest corner. "Lash and...." Hargold swept around the boarded up storefront to get an angle on the second sign. "Ah, Thorn. Good."

"Cozy combination. You recognize where we are?"

"We're about five minutes walk from the carry."

"No, we're not."

"What are—"

I shook my head and pointed. "Maybe your buddy the loan shark isn't so bad."

Thief followed the finger to where his unit was parked across the street. "How thoughtful of him to say something about moving it."

"Perhaps he assumed we'd just, you know, detect the presence of our carry," I said as we dodged a few carries on the way over. "Hey, bright side: I did."

"If they scratched the paint, you're paying."

"Idle threats. The pool will fix any damage for free."

Thief climbed in and started up the drive while I stowed the rod in the back. It took me a moment to shake out the coat. I frowned at the wrinkles and general vileness spattered on the wool. Making faces doesn't fix things though; I tossed the rumpled garment on the rear seat, doffed my hat, and got in the Hallowstone.

Despite the masochistic temptation to do so, I took care to not look down at the grime which doubtless clung to the legs of my pants; I also did my best to not think about the potential damage to the shoes I was wearing. Instead of further worry over clothing I settled my bubble.

"Nervous?" asked Hargold.

I felt the pressure of the restraint settle around me. "Not anymore."

"I don't mean about my driving. You seem to have a desire to be dumber than usual today."

My gut clenched. "What?"

"You're a better cop than this."

"So we ended up in a sewer, I mean—"

"No, not only that." He shook his head. "What were you thinking when you jammed a hand in your pocket back there?"

"I was going for—"

"Your sigil, yeah." He sighed and leaned in towards me. "They know we're cops, Griff. Even if they weren't already acquainted with me—or did you forget I'm only recently back with the HU? Even then—no humans go in there. Nobody else dresses like we do in Kaid's Cross. So why risk getting us killed to tell them something they're abundantly clear on?"

Heat rose in my cheeks. "All right, fine, sorry."

"Sorry won't help us if we're down on the Slabs." Thief waited, but I declined to comment. He pulled gracefully out into traffic, not making any sudden moves. I relaxed—a little bit anyway.

A few minutes later Hargold picked up the link and initiated a connection with dispatch to check on Cumberlan. The necromancer had called in his departure from the warehouse, but central didn't have him back at the Crypts yet. Given the congestion on the bridge they expected him to be slow coming across the Yarin.

Thief closed off with a request for a rundown on Crusher, then turned his attention to negotiating traffic in silence.

I was content to let him be. This was far from the first time I'd had my head torn off. The training officer assigned to keep me alive when I was new to the streets had run me up and down morning, noon and night. On the day she'd given me a final eval when we parted ways at six months she'd admitted I'd been the best new officer to come at her in ten years.

In Advanced Operator School I got crushed on a daily basis by the cadre of officers and senior enlisted personnel. The way they described me painted me as the single worst Lieutenant they'd ever had the displeasure of being saddled with. Yet I had graduated with honors, and even spoken at the final ceremony.

Still, I wasn't sure how such matters worked with detectives. We were expected—to a certain extent anyway—to already comprehend what being a detective entailed. By the time we hit the streets as a D3c we were over twelve months on the Job. Plus we'd studied, taken the exam, and finished the 80 day Advanced Investigations Course.

Even then, I'd be chained to a senior partner for at least a year. Regs prohibited third classes from any unsupervised outings. To help drive that point across new detectives weren't issued a unit until they got the second class bump.

Potentially worst of all, there was no guarantee I'd ever make D2c. Part of who made the decision was the currently pensive Detective First Class Hargold Thief. His recommendations—or condemnations for that matter—with regards to my aptitude would be studied and considered by the promotions board.

Past performance is no guarantee of future results. I'd learned the phrase during my platoon commander days. Oddly enough I'd never contemplated the fact that I might run into a job I was not suited for.

"What's on your mind, Dire?" asked my partner as we idled at an intersection.

I glanced over at him. My stomach tensed. "If you'd give me a list of things idiots do, I could avoid them."

He laughed. First I'd heard him do so genuinely, not for effect. The sound was rich, deep, and strangely warm. "List would be too damned long. Not even you're smart enough to memorize all those pitfalls."

"Glad I amuse you."

"It's my job to bust your balls, newbie. One day, if I do it right, you'll get some wet behind the ears D3c to crush beneath your heel."

"Sounds...fun."

"Oh believe me, the look on your face is worthwhile." He accelerated as the light changed. "Seriously. Stop trying to get us killed."

"Fair enough. Where are we going?"

Thief grinned. "Downtime while we wait on a profile of our suspect and anything Dermit finds when he gets the body to the Slabs. We're getting some food."

"Brilliant."

The smile vanished—in a manner which suggested it wouldn't be reappearing any time soon—and he turned towards me as he wove through traffic faster and faster. "And I'm going to force you to list all the idiot things you've done today. Or you don't eat."

I tightened my grip on the seat and hoped we'd make it to brunch.

CHAPTER 5

Patrol officers have a lot of misconceptions concerning detectives. Even more about those assigned to the specialty postings like Homicide Unit. My first day in the HU was as far from expected as you can get. Case in point—what happened while we relaxed at the diner.

We managed to shovel some food in our bellies—though I did have to wait until after I'd listed my sins—but we hadn't finished before the info on Crusher came back. Not from dispatch, as expected, but from a handful of detectives who piled into the booth with us, unceremoniously interrupting our repast.

The lead officer was a Detective Sergeant, name of Yamah. She was older than Thief, and certainly no less haggard for her years on the Job. Her squad consisted of a first class and two seconds. Bale, Kinsley, and Argova made an imposing trio. Each of them fell between Hargold and myself in height. Bale even seemed to out-mass Thief.

Yamah had finished her introductions and slapped a box of files down in front of us. We got invited to dig in and read up on the Tyrants. Thief started with the file on Crusher—conveniently located atop the pile—but it was thin. Took me less than five minutes to absorb every last word once he passed the dossier over. The rest of the box proved to be crammed full of jackets on the gang's members, suspected crimes, habits, and more.

They were, to a man, unpleasant. Their initiations required a crime worthy of a Dunsmire sentence. If the Goblin Court is mostly harmless, the TNO was anything but. The gang pushed the majority of the drugs in the ward, and violently enforced their collective will.

An hour after they arrived I'd gotten curious and asked Yamah why they'd come to see us in person with all the extra weight. In the queerest way her smile reminded me of my mother's—warm, gentle. Completely at odds with her entrance.

"OCU made things worse by taking out the old leadership," she'd said to me as she stirred sugar into a cup of coffee. "The hole was filled by someone far more vile than anyone anticipated." She'd jerked her head at Thief. "HU pissed off the new boss. Bad enough that she came back to New Dagonia and took the Tyrants over."

Crusher hadn't been seen in seven years. The file indicated that the city-state became unpleasant for her after a botched bank robbery. "You figure she returned because of Goran," I'd said.

Yamah had nodded and tapped the cup with her spoon to shake the drops off it. "Now you've got a body, and it's not just another scumbag. Rumor has it this time you might even have the corpse of someone big enough to care about. So, if it is, we'll get the CoD's go-ahead to raid them."

"Why not before?" I'd asked, though I'd suspected I already knew the truth.

"We're just here to keep the violence from spilling out into the city proper," she'd said. A sad look had appeared on her motherly face. "As long as they kill each other—or do in addicts, prostitutes, and the like—we're under orders just to close the cases that solve themselves."

"And nobody talks."

"So everybody walks."

I'd nodded and gone back to reading. The Tyrants changed for the worse after the previous leadership went down in an OCU sting. The gang's violence prior to that had been regular, and unpleasant, though nothing in the files pointed to a history of the type and frequency of extreme acts becoming commonplace.

Crusher seemed out for vengeance.

But before now, as she'd pointed out, very little had been directed against anyone not already in a death spiral. With resources slim Kaid's Crossing, Black Spit, and a few of the other wards became such low priorities they almost didn't register.

Mid-afternoon the wyrm turned. Cumberlan's voice came across the link and confirmed the way Goran killed his victim as identical to the manner in which our vic died. He also identified our body.

His name was Haydar Blane. Lived in Archstone. Married. One kid. Missing three weeks.

The big news was that Blane was a Senior Shift Supervisor at Dunsmire Keep, Goran's home for the next two plus decades. He held information about—and access to—the entirety of The Crag. Pass codes—and a set of keys—were within his purview.

Yamah jumped on her link to the Chief of Detectives' office before Thief broke the connection to the Crypts. She pushed for—and got—authorization and resources to go after Crusher and the Tyrants based on the imminent threat of a breakout attempt. Warrants for every known member were authorized on the basis of conspiracy to liberate the incarcerated.

Our reinforcements met us in a staging area a quarter mile from the location we were targeting. The cavalry in this case took the form of half of RRU2—four Rapid Response Unit squads—as well as a Sky Eye surveillance golem from the Airborne Tactical Unit.

A bit of wrangling and intervention by our Captain ended in me donning a hauberk and helm, arming myself with the rod, and waiting in an alley a half block from the main TNO hangout. The scummy bar and dance club occupied most of an otherwise abandoned set of buildings.

"Hard to believe these guys don't have any neighbors, huh?" I asked anyone who was listening.

Thief poked me in the back of the head under my helmet. "Smart ass. Your rod ready to go?" I didn't bother to check it again. It was as ready as any of us.

As the winter light faded away on my first day as a homicide detective, Detective Sergeant Yamah's voice sounded over the link.

"All ready teams: go," she said. "Hit the bastards hard."

Thief scurried behind me as I followed the Rapid Response Unit Corporal and his partner out of the alley and along the sidewalk. The four of us were tasked with assaulting the side entrance eighty feet away. Two full RRU teams had the main door; another was in the rear. Yamah's squad—which I'd discovered were actually Kaid's Cross watchtower detectives, and not specialists—were all holding in their units; ready to back any of the three prongs up, or chase down runners with the ATU golem's assistance. With them were the last two RRU officers: the Lieutenant and a Corporal, who kept distance to help coordinate.

"Breach in ten," said Yamah's disembodied voice as we hustled to make our point of entry. Our uniforms flanked it while Thief and I stacked up against the wall behind the officer.

"Breach," she said.

The Corporal swung the door open and swept in and to the left. His partner moved on his heels, turning right. As we followed I pressed towards the Corporal, deep into the room; Thief did the same in the opposite direction. I slipped through a rotten floorboard and stumbled in the gloom, but made it to my corner; rod raised and ready.

Shouts came from the front of the building, piercing the exit next to me. "Clear," I said. Three echoes answered. I announced my surroundings. "Door."

"Hallway," said the officer behind me.

Before the Corporal called out his next command I heard footsteps and stepped away from the portal. Weapons began to discharge throughout the structure. I barely had time to report, "incoming," as I took another step back.

Shouts and the exchange of volleys out front became even more apparent as the door burst open and Tyrants streamed in.

"Drop it," I shouted at the lead gang member. He turned and raised his wand. "Drop—"

Thief's weapon discharged, catching the youth squarely and sending him flying into the corner where he lay still. I fired on the second Tyrant and caught a chunk of the third in the rod's cone. Both of them went down screaming.

Blasts started to come in through the doorway at random. The Corporal shouted as he fell, dropping his rod. He clutched his left leg with one arm and pulled his backup with the other. The wall behind him was set ablaze by flame blasts, and peppered with ice and earth. "Hallway," he said, and began to return fire.

Thief slid across to my rear. I crouched and inched up to the opening, adjusting the crystal's band to a medium spread. I waited, steadying my breathing, readying for an opportunity.

He tapped my helmet.

I moved forward and brought my rod to bear on the Tyrants in the hall. My first discharge rained shards of earth throughout the corridor, catching the most brazen of the crew trying to storm our position and throwing him backwards through a doorway.

The report of Thief's wand sounded just above my head. Lances of ice caught the arm of another gang member, forcing him back into cover.

A meaty, green fist flashed out from behind an opening on the right side of the hall. A black object spun towards us, then whistled by, landing in the corner next to our downed man.

"Orb!" The RRU Corporal kicked it back at the open door then covered up. I felt weight come down on me. Hargold's fist gripped my hauberk and we rolled backwards. The rod discharged into the ceiling; we collapsed into a heap.

Intense light and noise filled the room. I shook my head and fought my way to my knees. Bile rose in my throat as equilibrium became a thing of the past. I flicked my rod upwards and fired at the door.

I paused a second.

Discharged the rod.

Pause.

Discharge.

Hargold was yelling into his link. Someone—probably the other uniform—joined me in suppressing the doorway. Fire was being flung past my ear so close by that I couldn't be sure I wasn't in danger of wobbling into it.

The door frame was ablaze. Chunks flew out of the wall as my rod flayed the ratty wallpaper and plaster from it.

Fifteen shots in the crystal ran dry. "Reloading," I said, and dug into the hauberk's pouch for a spare.

A cacophony tore through hallway. I dropped the rod and triggered the release on my wrist sheath. Twelve inches of icy death flicked into my hand.

Tyrants stormed in, wands blazing.

I caught the lead tough in the knee as I tracked the wand up. He went down in a heap.

Things got crowded quickly. There wasn't any cover to be had, so I remained kneeling in the center of the room, picked targets, and fired.

Three more of the gang fell—from my fire or the others', no way to tell—before I took a couple hits in the chest. The heavy impact knocked me away. I landed on my back; shook it off, and struggled to right myself.

I saw a massive middle-aged orc woman charging me, wand out. More Tyrants, armed and shooting at anything in their path, followed in her wake.

I got to one knee and swung the wand up, knowing I wasn't fast enough.

A fist caught me in the temple as I rose. Despite my helmet the world spun, and my wand skittered across the room as I slammed into the floor like a pole-axed steer.

"Dire!" The shout was meant to warn, but Thief had to know that no human could recover in time.

In that moment I let myself relax. As my iron control subsided, cracks formed in my essence. My totem beast surged into the void.

Then, in an instant, Dire was gone.

Only the griffon remained.

CHAPTER 7

I sat in the back of a chirurgeon's wagon with a blanket wrapped around me, sipping coffee. The street was filled with other wagons, patrol units, and—of course—the press.

Not every day a raid turns into such a spectacle.

The bulk of the bystanders were contained behind the cordons; but a few enterprising reporters had managed to get inside—probably by calling in favors—and were extracting information from anyone who would spare a moment to talk.

None of them had come near me-yet, in any case—but I'd seen Detective Sergeant Yamah get cornered a few minutes earlier. Hargold was nowhere in sight, which didn't concern me. I'd regained consciousness and the crew of the wagon had told me the score. Two RRU officers rushed away. No other serious NDPD casualties.

"Well, I managed to get you through day one."

I grinned, stifled the expression, then glanced behind me. Thief was perched in the front, tucked away from the street. "How long have you been here?" I asked.

"Someone let Birga through. I saw the idiot from the New Dagonia Herald and I needed to hide."

I nodded. She was forever making the cops she interviewed look like caricatures in her columns. "Nice of you to check on me."

"Happened to be the closest wagon."

"Uh-huh." I shook my head. "Bet Yamah was pissed she had to sit out."

Thief shrugged. "She cleaned up a big mess in her ward.

Chief of Detectives will give her a medal."

A pair of necromancers walked by, carrying another body bag. "Or fire her."

"Or that." He sighed. "Probably not though."

"You think they'll call this a win?"

"I don't know all that much. Most of the case belongs to Yamah; some will get kicked over to OCU. But from what I hear they're sifting through enough evidence of a plan to raid Dunsmire that the survivors are likely destined for permanent residence."

"No shit?"

"They were going to raid The Crag," he said. "Soon."

"Mad, mad plan."

"Speaking of madness—what exactly got into you?"

I swallowed hard. "Nothing."

"Bullshit, nothing. Never gamble, Dire. That might be the most obvious tell ever." He tapped a finger against his temple. "You got put down by an orc hopped up on all kinds of powders. Then got up—half a second later, if that—acting like she'd simply shaken your hand and kissed your cheek."

I can never remember much from the times my totem is in control. I shrugged. "Just doing my job. Heat of the moment."

"Your job consists of chasing down a pack of murderous gang toughs—unarmed, mind you—and eliminating them one by one?"

"Aye?"

"Followed by subduing said orc? Again—may I emphasize—without using any weapons?"

The longer I keep it chained up inside, the stronger the beast is when I let it free. I hadn't needed to give it control since the army, so I hadn't. "You said eliminate...."

Hargold ticked off fingers. "Broken ankle. Shattered knee. Busted collar bone."

"That's not so bad."

"I'm talking about the first guy. The others got worse. One of them may never walk again."

"Well, uh...."

"Listen, Griffon," said Thief as he slipped through the gap between the seats and the bay, "I'm your partner now." He tilted his head and narrowed his eyes. "You'd tell me anything I needed to know, right?"

I pondered the question.

He put a hand on my shoulder and squeezed. "I've seen you take people out before. I got enough of a look at you the night we met to know you can handle yourself."

"Oh aye, I remember you telling me what an idiot I was."

He shrugged it off. "But tonight...tonight was something else."

I nodded.

"Please. Tell me, son."

"I'm...unusual."

"Oh really?"

"I'm being serious, Thief."

"Sorry, go on."

I sucked in a deep breath and scanned the scene. Nobody was paying attention to the homicide detectives tucked inside a wagon. "I'm a natural talent. A wizard." I rushed to get the words out. "Here in New Dagonia they call people like me prodigies and send us to special schools."

"Why join the army, or the department?" A softness crept into the question. "Why waste that talent?"

"How many hours have I been a detective?" I gestured towards the chaos of the scene. Another body bag was being carted out of the building. An armored lorry sat loaded with survivors cleared for processing.

"Right. Point taken."

"So part of my power is—well, protection."

"Some kind of magical guardian thing?"

I nodded. He was perceptive. "Close enough."

"Well, whatever it is, thank it if you see it. Saved me a lot of paperwork. Losing your partner day one is about a hundred forms." He hopped down out of the wagon. "Speaking of which, someone is waiting for us in the carry."

The blanket hit the deck as I shrugged it off and downed the coffee. "I think I might enjoy doing the paperwork on her."

"You can be my guest. She's your collar after all, Detective Dire."

We walked towards the carriage where Crusher awaited our pleasure. Right then, in the chill of the night—on the streets of a ward we were leaving a safer place—I realized how good that title sounded.

I was Detective Third Class Griffon Dire, New Dagonia Police Department, and it was my job to catch killers.

I liked my job.

NOON HIGH

CHAPTER 1

Detective chic is—as always in Homicide Unit—the uniform of the day, so showing up in the bull pen wearing a freshly pressed set of grays is like rolling in honey and expecting flies to leave you alone.

Falcon is the first to rib me. "Don't you look lovely?" He turns to Calaran. "Doesn't he look lovely?"

The other Third Class grunts. No surprise there. He's two and a half years into his three year window for promotion, and he didn't even make board this quarter. Expecting him to be jovial when I'm barely past my required year as a detective is too much to ask.

Kif Falcon is a fresh D1c—and oblivious to his partner's pain—so he's not done messing with me. "What did they use on that thing? Those creases could cut someone." He narrows his eyes at me, but can't quite wipe the smirk off his face. "We get any calls on bodies shredded by unusual weapons and I'm putting a BOLO on you."

"I'm going for some coffee," says Calaran. He wanders off, and the veteran detective's eyes track him. I consider the fact that thinking of Falcon as too obtuse to recognize the other D3c's pain is unfair. He can see it. He just doesn't give a shit.

HU is one of the hardest specialist postings in the department. The simple truth of the matter is that Yane Calaran isn't good enough to make it, and we all know it.

Well. Except for maybe Calaran.

"So, come on. React, you bastard," Falcon says as he wiggles his fingertips at me.

I sit down at my desk and pull the official board summons out of the top drawer. The envelope is emblazoned with the full department seal. Dragon and all. I shudder slightly. I always do when I look too closely at the beast.

"Nervous?" Falcon's change of tone draws my attention. The ball-busting has given way to what passes for concern around this den of hard-cases.

"Not really. Excited, I guess."

He rubs the back of his head and smiles. "You damn well should be. Pretty amazing even getting a summons this early."

"Not everyone seems too happy."

"Fuck Calaran." He doesn't say it loud, but his vehemence is thunderous of its own accord.

I click my tongue. "Brother, he's your partner."

"So?" Falcon leans in across the aisle separating our desks. "I've been working my ass off for two and a half years to make him worth a good shit. At this point he's worth about two mouse droppings."

"He's not that—"

"Telling you, Griff, a rabbit could do better." He pauses and scans the pen, then slides over into the chair next to me. He lowers his voice further. "You know he managed to get fucking lost while canvassing a neighborhood last week?"

"Lost?"

"Seriously, he was gone for three hours." Falcon's face crinkles up. The effect is thoroughly unpleasant.

"Not answering his link?" I ask.

Third class detectives aren't actually allowed to stray from their partners during an investigation. Something as simple as splitting up to canvass isn't disallowed, of course. Uniforms ask routine questions on a daily basis; it's legwork, and when you need to cover ground you part ways for a while. But three hours unaccounted for is a problem for the senior partner, and there is a policy against being off link.

"He left it in my unit. On accident. He's 'sorry' and 'it won't happen again' if you can believe it...."

I make a noise. It's not pleasant. "Still, you've got to work with him."

"At this point all I've got to do is wait about six months until he's gone." He half smiles as he says it, but his face turns dark again almost immediately. "Unless he saves a council member's daughter from a serial killer."

"Well," I say as I stand up. "That's bloody likely."

"So I endure this horse shit," Falcon says, rising and moving back to his desk where an immense pile of paperwork lies stacked atop it.

I raise my coffee. "To stamina."

"To copious amounts of alcohol," he says, and kicks his bottom drawer.

"Whatever gets you through, Kif." Most of us keep a bottle or flask for late nights. I have a 20 year old whisky from Cannamore tucked in the back of my cabinet which is destined to be shared if I make second.

"Just wait until you get to break a tough one in." He sighs and sinks into his chair. "I hope I'm there to see the look on your face."

"I hope so too."

I pass Calaran on my way to the lift—I avoid stairs which will make me sweat when in dress uniform—but he ignores me. The snub is clear. At six-foot-three I'm too big to be missed.

As I start my descent into the bowels of Hammersmith watchtower, I spare a moment to follow the advice of *seanair*. I close my eyes and say a silent, but hearty, *fuck you* to my inept squad mate, then forget about him.

Granda had called it "getting the bad out" when I was a lad. He'd gotten his bad out loudly, and often; and he'd been a happy old bastard. Until the day the dragon ate him, that is.

"Reason enough to let shit go," I say to nobody in particular as the lift opened up to the garage and I headed for the venerable carriage I hoped to rid myself of with my promotion.

CHAPTER 2

Timberhold watchtower is huge. Most of the New Dagonia Police Department's facilities are imposing in their own right, but as the center of all department activity, Timberhold is unique.

Every one of the watchtowers is different, of course. Hammersmith is a single robust tower with a couple of outbuildings. My old haunt—Archstone—is a collection of low structures clustered around a slight spire.

Timberhold takes up most of three blocks and has a dozen towers, each with a number of edifices supporting it. The act of navigating the warren is a nightmare for the majority of officers on the force.

That's why I'm almost late for my board.

In this instance, 'almost' means I make it with three minutes to spare. For someone as punctual as I am the results are a racing heartbeat and compulsive checks of my chrono to make sure I'm still what other people think of as on time. 9:27AM hovers above my palm as I—only slightly winded from my speed walk—approach the small reception area located outside the appointed conference chamber.

My partner has a go at me regularly on the subject of how effortless my timely nature seems. The truth is that it's a lot of effort to work out exactly how long things take. Then you're stuck forcing yourself to account for a small enough margin of error. Otherwise you're risking showing up an hour early everywhere you go; huge waste of time if you make a mistake. Ruins the effort if you err the other way.

I do a circle around the wooden chairs and benches as I breathe in and out. I slow down each lap; both my breathing and my pace. My pulse and respiration are normal when the doors to the room open and D1c Hargold Thief walks out.

He's the reason I joined the force, and I was lucky he became my mentor when I was assigned to HU. Hargold is bigger than I am, but not taller. When I describe him as a bear, that's doing him a disservice. He's much more terrifying than any real bear, and tremendously more calculating.

His grizzled and graying blond hair is tamed, his beard is trimmed, and he's wearing his most conservative suit.

"Morning, Griff," he says. "Looking sharp."

I run a hand down my body. "This is required." I tilt my head and raise an eyebrow. "What about you? Fancy, fancy."

"Me?" His eyes widen. He's toying with me.

"No, no, I get it." I put on the most earnest face I can manage. "You hate driving me around with every ounce of your soul, don't you?"

"It's true." He nods. His visage transforms into a mask of tragic grief. "I told them you were utterly incompetent, but I begged them to promote you just so you'd have your own ride."

"At least you didn't need to lie."

His face goes less joking brother, more kindly father, and I know what's coming. "Chin up, eyes bright. Keep addressing the board members as you answer. Don't make all my pretty words go to waste."

I nod. Saying anything would ruin his gesture, so I don't. My chrono sounds.

The door opens. "Detective Dire?" asks a young man in a dark blue suit.

"Aye."

"The board will see you now."

I bob my head to Thief and walk across to the doorway. He gives me the slightest of smiles as I glance back. Then I cross the threshold of the chamber where I'm about to state my case before the seven people who hold the key to my promotion.

I step out of the meeting room almost an hour later. I'm sweating, and I feel sick. The questions launched at my by the board had been rapid fire, delivered in perpetually disapproving tones, and—worst of all—were far from straightforward.

"Congratulations! I can tell you've done well."

I look up to see Hargold, hold back another tremor, and narrow my eyes in his direction. "Oh?"

"I came out of my first board and promptly threw up." He points at a rubbish bin down the hallway. "Right in the trash." He makes a disgusting sound. I get queasy.

When the wave of nausea passes I struggle with the incongruity of Thief being phased by anything, let alone a room full of administrators. "You're kidding."

"Wish I was, kid." He rubs his brow. "They really sweat you in there, huh? I remember this one ancient bastard—used to be a uniform long before I joined—who kept going on and on about procedures. Arrest, interrogation, canvassing, blah, and bleah."

I manage a weak laugh. "Maybe he has a little brother."

"Nah, that guy is positively juvenile compared to the one who nailed me." He shakes his head. "Figures though. Your guy—Samora—he was a Serial Crimes detective before he ended up here pushing endless papers in pointless circles."

"I think he learned something from interrogating serial killers." I suck in a deep breath, then let it out slowly. "What're you doing waiting on me?"

"I brought you two things." He reaches back and pulls a familiar duffel off the seat. "First, a change of clothing." He hands me the *just-in-case* bag I keep in his unit.

"What's the second?" I ask as I unhook the buttons and begin pulling my spare suit out.

"A fresh homicide."

CHAPTER 3

"What the...," I say as I step into the apartment. Hargold grunts. "Damn." The simple curse is the only word to escape his lips before we start our sweep of the scene.

The victim is lying on the floor face down, pants around his ankles. A necromancer named Greene is crouched over him performing tests. A handful of others a crowded into the combined living and dining area. There are a pair of uniforms I've never met and a trio of Deductive Magic Unit specialists; two of whom I've never met and a third I'd rather not have.

Blood is everywhere inside the cramped apartment. Spatter from the impact. Castoff from the weapon. Pools. Footprints scattered across the room.

Even the better part of a palm print, stark against the white archway I'm standing in. So fresh I can see the crimson waves where it's started to go tacky. I raise my hand to the imprint. The mark on the wall is tiny in comparison to my large hand, situated low, and wrapped around the corner.

Spray coats the framed illuminations on the wall to my right. Most of them have been coated with a fine mist, or huge drops, or both. They're of a human man and woman, as well as a girl strikingly similar in appearance to the woman. The adult female isn't in the newer pictures, and the girl only seems to be happy in the older ones. The recent illuminations are also marked by an odd expression on the man's face.

A large image with informal composition shows the three mugging for a picture on a bench in front of a river. It appears to be one of the last pictures where all of them are together.

"Divorce?" I ask the room. Half a dozen non-committal grunts and shrugs answer me.

"Who called the massacre in?" asks Thief. "We get lucky and score a curious neighbor?"

"Yeah," says the junior uniform. "She's number fifteen. Left down the hall. Her name is—" He pauses and reaches for his notebook.

"Buttercup," says his partner, a Corporal. "Tali Buttercup. She's being watched."

Thief nods. We go back to our sweep; the neighbor will wait.

All the usual furnishings are spread across the area. A small table with three chairs is pressed up against the wall near the kitchen exit. There are a couch and a recliner. The seating is accompanied by a low—and blood-soaked—table which borders on the open space the body is lying in. On the opposite side of the room is a modest tapestry. The device is displaying a popular daytime drama play; something about chirurgeons and their love lives.

"Corporal Flyn, help me roll him," says the necromancer. The uniform bends down and the two of them flip the man over.

My jaw drops open. A retching noise hits my ears. Thief and I half shout a chorus of, "puke outside!" Flyn's partner flees the room holding both of his hands over his mouth.

Wet, sickly sounds drift in from the hallway as the rest of us stare at the man. I contemplate joining the patrol officer but decide it wouldn't look professional. Instead, I focus on an assessment of the mangled corpse.

While the back of the body had been clearly brutalized, the front side of him is testament to what can only be described as an overt manifestation of his killer's extreme rage.

He's been stabbed. Repeatedly.

Dozens of wounds cover him. His open shirt has been cut up a bit, but mainly the tracks of the weapon are evident on the exposed center of his body.

Extreme damage extends well beyond his torso. The victim's face has been removed. Hacked to bits. Not a professional job; rather what amounts to an obliteration of his features.

Yet the worst is what had been done to his groin. I ache just from looking at the mess his killer made.

His penis is missing, as are his testicles. A huge hole exists between his legs; carved out of the flesh where his sex organs once resided.

"Damn," Thief says.

"Someone hated him." I shake my head. "I mean really hated him."

My partner nods and blows out a quick blast of air. His brow rises and falls, and his stoic mask returns. "Greene?"

"Detective." The necromancer responds from his position just over the mutilated corpse. His eyes are glazed over.

"Tell us if you find anything we need to be aware of."

Greene nods. We walk out and I'm in the lead. Not that it matters; we both know where we're going next.

We sit waiting for Tali Buttercup to prepare some tea. The uniform keeping her company is working on his third cup. He's not shy about asking for more or complimenting her on the brew. I figure it's either good tea, or he happens to be sweet on her.

Buttercup is young; a bit on the mousy side, but otherwise attractive. This uniform isn't wearing a wedding band. A lot of cops like marriage. Most can't maintain one. Somehow that fact doesn't deter their wishful thinking.

Her apartment is slightly larger than our victim's. It's also neat. Extremely organized, in fact. Her books are alphabetized. A once-over tells me she reads a lot of mysteries. Idle thoughts about what a fiction buff must think when they're thrust into a familiar role cross my mind.

I banish them as she offers me a cup and saucer. Thief and I both thank her.

"Miss Buttercup," I say as she sits across from me, taking a position next to the uniform on the couch. "Would you please tell what transpired before you called the police?"

"I heard screaming." She bites her lip. "Mr. Jemah was screaming."

"How did you know it was Mr. Jemah?" asks Thief.

"Well, I didn't then." She frowns. "Not when I called. Not until later."

"So you heard a man screaming."

"Yes. But it didn't even sound that much like a man. Almost like an animal." She shudders. "It was awful."

I take a sip of the tea and grimace. Thief continues his questions. "What made you think it was Mr. Jemah?"

"Oh, Luzi ran by my door." She shakes her head and sobs. "Poor girl must have found him. She was covered in blood." The uniform scoots closer to her.

I bobble my tea as I set it down. It clatters on the saucer. Hargold flicks his eyes over at me as I shrug. "Who is Luzi?" I ask.

She answers as I wipe tea off my hands with a napkin from the pretty little tea service. "Luzi Jemah. She's Mr. Jemah's daughter. His name is Tad, you know. Well, no, Tadwin."

"And Mrs. Jemah is where?"

"Oh, she died. Before I moved here. So terrible. Another senseless carry accident. That's why I take the train."

"Aye. Awful. And wise of you. Now, did you see anyone else in the hall?"

"Someone walked by a few minutes before the screaming. Heavy footsteps, but I was watching the tapestry before work." She starts to wring her hands. "I feel just awful, detectives. I'm sure I could have seen whoever did this to him if I'd only peeked."

"I see." I tap my finger on the tabletop. "You heard heavy

footsteps, a lot of screaming, and you called emergency services. Then you got up and looked through your peephole. That's when you spotted Luzi Jemah running?"

"Yes."

"How long after the screams started was that?" Thief asks.

"Just a few minutes. Maybe five?"

My partner and I share a look. "Miss Buttercup, do you know what Luzi was wearing? Was she carrying anything?"

She describes the girl. Thief excuses himself and heads out into the hall. I glance at the uniform's sigil.

"You know, Miss Buttercup, if you're concerned for your safety I could have an officer stay with you for a while."

"Oh. Would you?"

"Absolutely. You'd be able to remain posted here and protect our witness this afternoon, wouldn't you, Officer Neph?"

He shoots me what I take to be a grateful look. "Of course, Detective."

"I'll call dispatch and let them know we're looking out for you. Thank you again for your cooperation." I stand and try to tip my hat to her but remember that I don't have one today. I settle for a tug on my forelock and wish the gesture didn't make me look like I grew up in the backwater I did.

Neph stands and walks me to the door. He puts a hand on my arm, stopping me from leaving. "Thanks, Detective, but how did you guess I wanted an excuse to loiter?"

My eyebrow rises of its own accord. "That tea is rubbish."

I make an exit as he considers my words.

CHAPTER 4

We're barely back in the unit when we get the call. The BOLO Thief put on Luzi Jemah trips a snooper at the Rigger's Square NDUT terminal. The transit cop on the link tells us that the automaton spotted her leaving the station five minutes earlier, headed south.

We listen to the description spilled by the construct. Everything matches. The drone even reports that the subject's shoes are stained red.

Thief pauses for half a second before he mashes the accelerator, sending the Hallowstone surging through the tight late-morning traffic. I hit the lights and call for backup. Rigger's Square is a straight shot on the underground from the Jemah place. The snoopers aren't always right, but I'm glad the pieces add up this time.

I check my chrono as our speed causes us to scrape across the cobblestones of an uneven intersection. 11:38AM.

We pick up an escort about halfway to the station. The patrol unit clears three intersections for us before they fade away, blocked by a lorry. I don't envy the citation the driver is bound to receive.

I kill the shock and awe before we get too close to the underground. Sirens are hardly rare in New Dagonia, but I don't want to scare our quarry off. If Luzi is our killer, she's clearly unpredictable.

Thief starts to work his way around the square. The link fires up again. An undercover hackney unit has our suspect in sight at the Yarin, not even two blocks away. I order them to observe and report.

Thief grits his teeth. I reckon he's trying not to say something sarcastic about the coppie. By virtue of his posting, the hackney detective is at least a Second Class. It wouldn't matter if he were a Lieutenant, of course. Homicide Unit has tactical command during the pursuit of persons of interest in a murder investigation.

Only SCTF and RRU can pull jurisdiction in our bailiwick with any kind of impunity. Even at that, unless we're chasing a serial murderer or something indicates a severe public safety threat, nobody gets in our way. HU is close to the top of the NDPD food chain. Murder is taken extremely seriously in New Dagonia.

So, my case, my call. The detective confirms my orders. He informs us that our subject has just entered Twilling Park, and indicates that they've left their cab and are proceeding on foot.

I get dispatch on the link and report the girl's location. Within seconds all of the officers en route know where she's gone. Thief parks the Hallowstone and we jump out. I'm into the park before he can even get around the vehicle.

In total we have the hackney unit, the four EMU patrol officers—and their mounts—normally assigned to Twilling, four patrol units from the surrounding area, and the two of us from HU. Falcon calls in to report that Calaran has gotten them stuck in Hammersmith traffic and they won't make it downriver to Timberhold for another ten minutes or more. Thief decides to go without them.

It's just one girl against sixteen officers.

Luzi Jemah is sitting on a park bench between the carousel and the observation tower, staring out at the boats floating up and down the Yarin. I get momentarily dizzy as I make the connection to the illustration in her apartment. My mind races, trying to imagine what she's thinking.

This is a place with happy memories. I remember the carefree smile on her face as she hangs on her parents shoulders over the back of the bench.

But I can also see the crimson on her shoes—and hands—from my position.

I'm not even forty feet away, reading a newspaper I grabbed out of the first bin I encountered. Something sticky and foul-smelling is running down the pages, but I need the camouflage. Even the least observant people get excitable when their blood is up.

Nothing like murder to get the blood up.

I'm off link because I'm closest to the girl, but I've marked Thief busily coordinating the others from behind a Parks Department grounds keeping lorry. I flip to the next page of the rag and feel the stickiness drip on my pant leg.

Luzi stands up and walks away from me. I crease the paper and stand then wiggle the folds to catch Hargold's eye. He peeks out and resumes rattling off orders on the link.

Things go wrong fast as one of the Equestrian Mobility cops can't back his mount away quickly enough. I can see the horse's ass through the trees, and Luzi catches sight of its head. Only EMU is allowed to ride here. Their presence is a dead giveaway.

The girl bolts towards me.

I try to duck my head, but I'm too close; too conspicuous. She takes one look at me and marks me for what I am. Arms and legs pumping wildly, Luzi heads towards the observation tower at a flat out run.

My stomach clenches and I hesitate. At the top of the spire her options for escape don't exist. She's treed herself, and it makes me uneasy. Cornered rats spring to mind.

I jerk the link free of my coat pocket. "All units, stand by. Maintain your distance. Subject has entered the tower."

"Dire, what's your plan?" Thief asks. His voice comes across the void and the rapidly diminishing space between us as he closes on me.

I turn and face my partner. "She's got nowhere to run."

"How many do you want to take with us?"

I wrinkle my brow. "Isn't that your call?"

"Yeah." He nods. "How many?"

I get on the link and order all of our backup to maintain station except for the coppies. I give them the task of watching the tower's entrance at close range as Thief and I head up. Less than a minute later we're ready for our ascent.

The tower has a steep set of stairs and a single car lift. Thief hops on the conveyance and waves as I mount the staircase. I keep my head up and trust my balance to carry me up the flights. Better to trip on the steps than catch a knife in the face around one of the blind corners.

I don't trip by the time Hargold signals me that he's up top. Luzi is young, but nobody could make the climb in two minutes. We know she's between us without exchanging a single extra word.

My climb continues. I know the girl has a lead on me, and that Hargold will have to deal with her alone for however long it takes me to make my way up. I press myself harder.

Every flight I pass a series of tiny slits in the wall. The arrow loops are left over from when the tower was part of the Twilling Ramparts, a river defense fort that's been gone for over a hundred years now. The light from outside streams in through the holes and mingles with the globes mounted on the walls. The effect is something akin to twilight. The atmosphere is eerie and unnerving, but Hargold needs backup.

Worry for my partner is my undoing. Legs on fire from sprinting, I slip and miss a tread. Catching myself before I smack my face into the ground, I feel a twinge in my left wrist and pain shoots through it. "Bugger me," I say, and cradle my injury as I roll onto my arse.

I only spare a moment for the pain as I find myself staring down the treads. I notice a few stray lines of light coming from the external wall just below. I try to clear my vision by shaking my head, but I'm not injured that way; what I see is real. There is light leaking into the tower from a small door, no more than three feet high.

I move down a bit and lose the light again. It's only visible from the right angle, and when you climb the steps you're only at that exact angle for a moment.

"She there yet?" I ask over the link, my voice low.

"Negative. I had one couple pop out up here just after we spoke. Still no sign of her."

I continue to whisper. "I have an exterior door and I'm checking it out."

"What? Exterior...Griff, don't you d—"

I silence the link.

Concentrating for a few seconds, I loose my spirit. The totem gathers ley energy—abundant next to the Yarin—and returns it to me. I kindle a soft light in the palm of my hand and examine the edges of the portal.

The door in front of me is roughly square and appears to open out into nothingness. At the base of it is freshly displaced dirt. A bent pin is lying two treads down, and the latch meant to be held secure by the hunk of metal is undone. The door itself rocks gently back and forth as wind off the river presses in against the tower.

I debate pulling my weapon, but I decide to keep the wand up my sleeve for the moment. It's likely to be unwieldy outside, and if Luzi is close to the opening I might scare her needlessly.

With feet resting against the door I apply gentle pressure. The egress swings open without much effort, flooding the steps with light.

At my command the spirit moves away from me again, out and free into the skies it belongs to. I focus on guiding the beast back to look at the tower. It struggles against me, eager to fly. To soar. To hunt.

This last desire is the one I hold fast to, pouring the image of Luzi through the ethereal tether joining us. She is the object of my hunt, and it can sense me stalking her. Our bond rouses its instincts, and it rushes back towards the spire.

Circling high above, swooping across the face, it scours the tower. The totem barely exists in the physical realm thanks to my control. The spirit cannot so easily discern the inhabitants of my world, but I impose my will on it, and the beast's focus narrows sharply.

The griffon's attention snaps to the girl clinging to the tower, just a bit more than halfway up. The totem scents her fear across the gulf between dimensions, and screeches a hunting challenge which I alone can hear.

I ram myself into the beast. For a second I am disoriented, adrift above the river on air currents. I recover and settle in, then look at her.

Luzi Jemah clings to the tower like an insect. She's found a way to move across the tower to the opposite side using the putlog holes. The holes are deep enough for her to fit her feet into as they once supported the wooden hoardings which offered the tower's garrison a better field of defense. Now she's high above the ground on the river side, digging her hands into the rough hewn stones and crying.

I thrust myself free of the totem, ride the silvery cord back down, and slump into my mortal coil. Even as I struggle against the momentary sadness the break causes, I recall the beast. The spirit returns and I feel it—grudgingly—slip inside. Worry falls from my shoulders; I sigh and relax.

After a moment I take a deep breath in and let it out again. Twice more, slower each time.

Then I push myself out through the door and into the empty space beyond.

CHAPTER 5

Wind whips at my clothes; gusts tear at my spare coat, tug at my slacks, and bite into my cheeks. I almost reach for my hat before I remember leaving the fedora at home this morning.

I glance down. My gut roils with vertigo. As a lad I fell from perhaps half as far, and even landing in water I all but died. I find myself frozen as I realize it's been nearly three years since I've scaled anything.

My skills were honed on cliffs, trees, and glaciers. I was always scurrying up some object or the other as a littlin. Even after my fall, climbing was how I got away from fellow orphans—and our caregivers. When I'd graduated from university and joined up for the service obligated by my scholarship I could handle the Army's OAS obstacle course far more easily than the rest of the provisional lieutenants in my platoon.

Still, I'm at least a hundred fifty feet up and on this side only earth lies below me. I pull myself up and get settled in; my heart hammers and my mouth dries up.

I scoot around the tower using the putlog holes and gaps in the masonry as toe and hand holds. It's odd to climb again, and even stranger not to be burdened with an NDA platoon commander's loadout. As another gust of wind strikes me I wonder if the extra fifty or sixty pounds of my assault kit would help stabilize me.

The first corner is tricky. I swing my leg around and grope for the foothold. My stomach plunges as I search but can't find purchase. My palms start to sweat and I slip a touch as my left hand's grip falters.

The toehold is suddenly in reach; I jam my foot into the hollow and slide my body around. Luzi is somewhere past the next corner. If she hasn't fallen.

I hurry myself up, slithering across the stones as the noon sun beats down from above. As I traverse the section I'm torn deciding what's more stressful: the chance of being shot off a wall if a sentry spots you, or knowing that someone's life may depend on you getting to them.

The next corner is easier to navigate; I get my face around the edge quickly. The girl is still here, clinging to the pitted wall. She spots me immediately after I catch sight of her.

We face off for a moment. No words cross our lips as our eyes lock. Her dark pools meet my emerald orbs.

In an instant the spell is broken.

"Stay back!" Her tears stop and Luzi moves, putting a few more feet between us. "Keep away from me!"

"Luzi, my name is Griffon." I tip my head in greeting. I doubt the civility will matter to her, but options are limited up here. "I came to help you."

"You did not!" She screams into the wind. Tears roll down her cheeks again, only to be blown away. "Stay there! Don't touch me!"

"The ground is a long way down, Luzi. We need to get back inside where we can be safe." I keep my tone as low as possible, but I have to half yell for her to hear me over the gusts. Keeping calm while projecting your voice is hard; I feel like I'm scolding her. "Lets go talk."

"No!" She shakes her head so hard I'm afraid she's going to fly off the side of the tower.

"Look, nothing is going to happen if we head in. We'll talk about everything then." My left hand starts to shake. The injury to my wrist is starting to tell. "We're going to be ok," I say, and grunt as I shift a little, trying to ease the pressure.

"I killed him." The admission she makes is so quiet that I barely catch the words.

"I know."

"I fucking killed him!" Her eyes are huge as she shouts the confession.

"Aye, lass. Just come talk with me where it's safe." I'm keeping my voice as even as I can while clinging to the wall, but I don't like the direction things are headed. My wrist is close to giving out. Luzi is beyond distraught, and she's been out here longer than I have.

She shakes her head and sets her jaw.

"I just want to listen. You can tell me all about what happened. Why you killed him. I know you had a reason." We're not called on to negotiate often, but the basics are covered in the AI course. Training tells me to build rapport and trust.

I find that training is thrice-damned hard to find solace in when you're hanging over the bloody Yarin by your crippled wrist.

"There's a bunch of cops inside." Her statement isn't as angry; still, her eyes narrow, wary.

"Just me. I promise." I look up and give a slight jerk of my chin. "My partner is all the way up top, and he's old." I let her see a bare hint of a smile. "He won't be on the stairs, lazy bugger."

She stares at me for a few seconds. "You want to know why?"

"Aye."

"He raped me."

A chill goes up my spine; from the wind or the disgust, I'm not sure. "I'm sorry."

"Oh, you're sorry?" She laughs tears. "Every...single...day. For two years. Twice on weekends."

My mouth moves, but I fail to produce any sounds.

She screams at the top of her lungs. "My father raped me and I killed him!"

I'm stuck. No magic I can conjure up will deal with her growing hysteria. Even if I had a trick, I couldn't concentrate without risking falling.

"Luzi, I can't imagine how that must have felt." I'm not lying. I don't come into contact with victims of assaults often. I've dealt with a handful of rapes in my career, and only one since joining HU. Clinging to the side of a tower is where I live; the concept of an incestuous serial rapist may as well be the moon.

"No shit." She's not screaming now; just looks tired. My heart starts to hammer.

"Listen, I hurt myself, I'm starting to slip." The wrist trembles as I cop to it. "Can we please go? I'll follow you."

"Why? So you can be useless like everyone else? He had them all fooled."

"Who did he fool?"

"My counselor? My teachers?" She sobs uncontrollably and her face twists into a pain-etched mask. "You know what they said to me?"

"No."

"To stop acting out." She goes cold. Voice monotone. Eyes distant. "That my mother died two years ago and it was time to move on. That I should quit lying and do my homework."

I'm very nearly sick at the thought. I want to swear. I want to yell. I think of my partner's stoicism and lock those reactions down. "Luzi, please, come inside."

"I want it to be over."

"He's gone, lass. He can't hurt you."

"I'm free."

"Aye, you're free. Now come on, climb around; I'll follow." My hand slips and I clutch at the corner, digging into it with my whole body. I grunt as the impact rocks me. My right foot threatens to slide away as I force it to take the weight.

"Careful."

"Thanks." I shift and find a handhold again.

"We came here every chance we got. My mom and me. We were going to come the weekend she was killed."

"The view is beautiful" I nod into the distance behind her. "You can see the ocean."

"She loved the ocean. Loved the water. She was a swimmer."

"Let's go talk about her," I say, shifting again. My wrist is alternating between shooting pains and a maddening throb.

"Thank you...." She narrows her eyes and cocks her head. "Sorry, I forgot your name."

"Griffon."

"Thank you, Griffon." She smiles. "I'm free."

I scream as she jumps.

The sound is ripped wordlessly from my soul. I watch her plummet towards the Yarin and howl so loudly my voice obliterates itself in the end, trailing off into a rough, hoarse whine.

Her body strikes the water a few seconds later. I let the pathetic sound die as she disappears beneath the river's surface.

With my right hand I pull the link out of my pocket. My wrist protests against the extra weight as I flip the device back on.

"—mnit, Griffon, where are you?" Hargold demands, his voice high and tight.

"Here." I say.

"About damned time." More relief than anger. "What's going on?" Thief doesn't shake easily, but I've obviously rattled him.

"Get divers in the water. She jumped."

"Rescue?"

A tear startles me as it slips from my eye. The wind carries it away a moment later. "Recovery."

CHAPTER 6

I stand in a River Patrol boat with my arm in a sling, sipping coffee. The sun is starting to go down and they haven't found Luzi's body yet. The RP vessels were slow in getting to the scene.

I tell myself again the delay hadn't mattered. That she'd died on impact.

The tough sell comes as I try to convince myself I was imagining the moment when my totem swore we could fly. I push back the memory of the beast whispering to me as I screamed; urging me to soar.

I drain the coffee and set the cup aside.

My wrist is sprained. A chirurgeon had wrapped the injury for me while we'd waited on the water units. He'd informed me all I'd need were a few days of rest. I'd told him I would be sure to take the weekend easy. The response satisfied him; he'd released me.

I know my wrist will heal quickly; probably by the time I wake up Sunday morning. I've never been one to fall ill or stay hurt for long.

Physically, anyway.

Thief wanders up from below. "Damned tiny pisser."

"Aye." I'd gone to use the head before him and banged my forehead on two beams getting into the cramped closet.

"Any luck?"

I shake my head. We stare out at the river.

Bubbles rise from the diving crew. Three little collections of froth lie scattered across the surface of the Yarin. Three men search for the body of a girl driven mad by grief and betrayal.

"Just barely seventeen years old," says Thief, shaking his head.

"Too young," I say.

"To be a murderer?" he asks. We both know that's not true. We've seen killers of all ages. Goblins can get started very young indeed.

I suck in a deep breath and move to the railing. "I was thinking too young for the life she had."

"Shit." Hargold pulls his flask out and takes a swig. "Nobody is old enough for that hard of a life." He slides in next to me and extends the silver container.

"Aye." I take the drink and do more damage to the bourbon than just a swig.

"You've got to know it wasn't your fault. You did every last damned thing I can think of, Griff." He pauses and I hear his breathing. "You could've died."

I don't answer him. I'm not sure I did everything I'm capable of. The beast is restless inside. Its stirrings feel like an accusation of cowardice. I hit the flask again before handing it back.

My link flares to life. "072707. Dispatch. Central on line for you."

I look at Thief and he shrugs. My finger rocks the stud and I reply. "Dispatch. 072707. I'm go for central."

"Detective Dire, this is Captain Samora." He pauses, but I don't respond. Thief pokes me and mouths something.

I shake my head and wrinkle my brow. He starts to mouth the words again but the voice over the link continues. "I was the one drilling you this morning during your board."

"Oh, right," I say. "Sorry, I was...it's...been a long day."

"Ah, well, that's a shame, Detective. Just didn't seem right keeping you in suspense."

"Oh."

"I know how hard it can be, waiting on the board. It's all you think about. Better to get the results, even if they aren't what you hoped for."

I haven't given the board a thought since seeing the blood-spattered walls of Luzi's home. It seems impolitic to mention the fact to a Captain. "Aye," escapes my lips instead.

"Happily, I'm not going to give you bad news. Congratulations, Detective Second Class Dire."

It takes me a moment to find any words. When I do, they're succinct. Automatic.

"Thank you," I say. The words are hollow. I am hollow.

Thief takes my link, triggers the stud, and handles Samora. "That's wonderful news, Captain. I'll make sure he celebrates when we wrap up here." He slaps a huge grin on his face. It's forced, but serves to lighten his tone for the bureaucrat. "A big thank you from all of us at HU. Dire is a real asset, and I know our Captain will love the news. If you haven't already told him...."

"Of course, Detective Thief. I'll get in touch with him."

"Excellent. Thanks again, Captain. Off to finish up." He cuts the link and turns to me. "Griff—"

I shake my head and point.

We watch as a diver breaks the surface with Luzi Jemah's corpse.

I sink to the deck, grab hold of my knees and weep. My partner steps up behind me and puts his huge paw on my shoulder.

He doesn't let go until I'm done.

SUNSET RIDE

CHAPTER 1

When I go out, I want it to be like a lion.

Detective Sergeant Hargold Thief was all tussled hair and grizzled beard as he pounced into the bull pen and roared. It was Monday morning. The last Monday morning he'd report in for duty as a Homicide Unit detective.

I knew I'd miss him. We'd been partners for nearly six years. He'd gotten me to join the force after a chance meeting where I'd done something stupid enough that he figured I actually enjoyed putting my life on the line.

He hadn't been wrong.

Watching him bask in the adoration of the detectives and uniforms who walked the third floor at this hour of the morning made me wonder if I'd ever manage to do twenty-five years on the Job. Most cops took their twenty if they weren't already a Sergeant, but Thief had held on to twenty one, just hoping for the bump.

He'd earned it. He probably would have stayed on a year or two longer if it hadn't come then, but the need for three years at a rank to retire with full pension would have stopped him from trying before too much longer.

Of course my partner had been saying he was getting tired of it all since I'd first met him. For all I knew, he'd been saying it for his entire career.

But Hargold had earned his retirement. More than a quarter of a century had passed since Thief had put on the charcoal uniform. When my partner had set foot on the NDPD training grounds I'd been newly orphaned. His life in the barracks had coincided with my entry into the first of a series of institutions in the lowlands that I'd inhabited.

While no more suitable arrangement would ever be found for me, he'd been welcomed into the department and thrived. He started out as a uniformed patrol officer, made Corporal while a member of the elite Rapid Response Unit, and ground out all three classes of Detective as a Homicide Unit investigator.

When things got tough for the Social Crimes Division after a big Internal Investigations crackdown gutted the detective core, he'd gone on loan and bounced around, taking cases for both the Substance Abuse Unit and the Organized Crime Unit.

He'd finally settled back into Homicide Unit as primeshift's squad leader in the year before we became partners. Thief made Detective Sergeant right after I earned my Second Class. The timing of his promotion had been better than mine. So when he'd gotten the news I'd opened a bottle of Cannamore and we'd spent a weekend drinking the whisky—along with a bottle of bourbon, his preferred poison—to our shared success.

Now his run was drawing to a close, while I was headed into my prime years. I'd be eligible for First Class boards by the time another year passed.

But before then I would be put up on the market for a new partner. Which of course meant I risked being reassigned out of HU. Where the NDPD needs you, that's where you go. Hargold's stint at SCD hadn't been wholly voluntary; he complained about it readily enough when he'd had enough to drink.

Captain Trawler had started casually feeling me out with off-hand remarks over a month ago. Checking to see if I had any interests outside of putting killers behind bars. I was replaceable. There's always veteran watchtower detective partnerships willing to try their hand at homicide investigations if given the chance.

In an effort to ensure I was eating a full ration of shit each day, D1c Falcon had taken to sneaking up behind me and whispering the name of his washout partner in my ear. Back when Calaran was giving Falcon trouble day in and day out he'd cursed me with the hope that one day I too would have a new partner to break in. He was holding out for me being saddled with a pain in the arse newbie Third Class, fresh out of Advanced Investigations.

Even Hargold had gotten in on it. On Friday he'd taken me out, bought me drinks, and asked me what exactly I hoped I'd get in a new partner.

I was having none of it, and I wasn't shy about anyone knowing it. Trawler had been asked if drinking excessively counted as an interest. Falcon was still nursing his jaw from one smart remark too many. And Hargold had spent a lonely Friday evening after his question resulted in me pissing off out of our usual watering hole.

All I wanted was more time with the man I knew that I could trust with my life.

But there he was. Roaring and carrying on. Laughing—the genuine version, not the scathing sound used to abuse suspects and fellow officers alike—more than he'd managed in our entire partnership.

Hargold Thief was ready to retire.

Selfish bastard that I am, I wasn't ready to let him.

I'd just checked my chrono—marking it 08:55AM—when Captain Trawler worked his way into the crowd and made it clear that it was time to disperse. The good-natured arm flailing and barking which followed—mainly aimed at reminding us all that roll call was in ten minutes—was effective, without leaving anyone's spirits dampened. It was unusual to see the dwarf in such a good mood, but that didn't mean he was going to let his watchtower spend the entire morning celebrating Thief's impending departure.

Homicide Unit cops don't often retire. They usually just burn out. This means quitting, or putting in for a transfer to somewhere more relaxing. Like Robbery Unit. A lucky few get promoted up the line and exit through rank, at which point HU still considers them detectives emeritus. Trawler had been HU—and graveshift squad leader—before making Detective Lieutenant. Even though he'd moved over to Robbery Unit he was still considered to be one of ours.

Because of this churn the number of cops still working homicides at the end of their careers is minuscule. So, when a detective does make it all the way, tradition demands that they live out their final week with as little to do as possible.

Which of course means that the departing officer's partner is given a vacation at work as well.

Unfortunately for me, I had no desire to relax. With the time for my partner to bow out staring me in the face, I still wanted nothing more than to work another case with him.

My burning desire was compounded by the tedious nature of our last two weeks. We'd taken on three suicides, all easily cleared. The euthanasia we'd drawn would wind up in the courts for years—if not decades—to come, but wouldn't need any of our attention ever again. Boring.

And depressing.

It was nearly enough for me to wish a spectacular murder would appear. Something so intriguing that Hargold wouldn't be able to pass it up.

Of course that would mean someone dying, so I didn't really wish for it. Just idly daydreamed that a juicy case would drop in our laps.

So, instead of being out running down a murderer, Falcon and Thief were busy joking around, drawing dirty pictures on one of the blank murder boards. The senior detectives were clearly unwilling to let Trawler's orders related to doing something useful ruin the traditional final week festivities.

A fact which I'm sure would never have surprised the dwarf in a million years.

The clarion on Thief's desk chimed. He ignored it on account of being too busy drawing a very large penis on a man that looked suspiciously like himself.

Detective Second Class Bitholm Rabino—or Rabbit, also known as Falcon's other and better half—was the most junior member of the primeshift squad. That meant when one of us was ignoring a chime, he got stuck handling the clarion. The slender man dropped into Thief's extra chair, picked up, and said "HU, Rabino."

He listened for a moment before starting to scribble notes in his cramped hand. He confirmed the information being relayed to him in a low voice, and was off within a minute.

"We've got a body," said Rabbit after he'd dropped the horn and hauled himself out of the chair. He walked over to his desk and started grabbing his kit. He glanced over at me. "Clear homicide on this one, so we'll be gone a while. Looks like you get to take the calls."

"Hurrah," said Falcon as he finished drawing a busty mermaid with a flourish. "Looks like I win."

Thief shook his head. "You mean you forfeit."

"I'm ahead," said the detective. Bird split the age difference between Hargold and me, but was the least mature of the squad most of the time. He got under Hargold's skin all the time. They didn't hate each other though. They had more of a brotherly rivalry that spilled over into expletives and fists every once in a while.

"We've got time left." He jabbed a meaty finger at the chrono hanging on the wall.

"So? I win. Clear victor." He pointed to his collection of dirty doodles and looked to Rabbit and me for support. The rules of their game were too arcane for me to judge, so I just shrugged. His own partner pretended not to notice the glance.

"No way," said Thief. "This game hasn't run out. You walk out that door, you answer to 'loser' until the end of the week." He went back to his drawing.

"Come on, Kif," said Rabino. "Let the short-timer have his

way."

Falcon growled with a grin on his face and grabbed his coat. "Where we headed?"

Rabino checked the note. "Uh, Seaward. Gulls Court."

"Hold on," said Thief. "What's the number?" He'd abandoned what appeared to be an illustration of a filthy limerick to ask the question.

"357, 4D. Why?"

The curiously jovial Thief who'd been engrossed in his inappropriate artwork evaporated instantly. Nothing but the fierce, dangerous mask that my partner wore as part of his uniform of the day remained in the aftermath of his shifting mood. He ripped the piece of paper from Rabbit's hand. "That call is ours. Grab your gear, Griff."

My heart soared.

I'd regret the elation I felt at that moment by the end of the case, but in that second all I could think about was the fact that I had another chance to ride with my partner.

"Oh yes, Bird-n-Prey get to sit this one out," I said, doing a little dance as I went for my duster.

"Knock it the fuck off, Dire." I froze as Thief's words hit me. "Sorry," he said, shaking his head. "Hurry it up though, we need to go."

I hurried past the other two detectives and followed the broad backside of my mentor towards the lift. He was moving faster than usual and even half jogging I still trailed in his wake.

The last thing I heard as we left the bull pen was Rabino asking Falcon a pointed question. "So, Kif, you going to call him 'loser' when he gets back?"

CHAPTER 2

Complete silence between us was a rare thing. Unless one of us was unconscious—or being punished—chatter in the unit tended to have a regular ebb and flow when we were out on a call. So the complete lack of conversation as we made our way to Seaward was disconcerting. I was taking a long, hard look at my eagerness to catch a final case by the time we pulled up in front of Gulls Court 357.

Thief sat for a moment after I parked my unit. He drummed his fingers on the Hallowstone's console and stared out the window at the steps. The cordon which arced between the railings was being watched by a uniform.

I didn't make a move to get out. Partly because I was afraid of what Hargold might do to me if I broke whatever spell he was under. Partly because I wanted him to take the lead, for old-times sake. I let my eyes scour our surroundings instead. Mostly to keep my thrice-damned mind off worrying about him.

Residences in Seaward had changed from the purview of the wealthy into bastions of middle-class existence some time in the last hundred years. I'd never known the ward to be anything but filled with families and professionals living their lives; with the few remaining wealthy being consigned to the dwindling affluent sections of the ward.

Gull's Court was all converted from huge gentleman's homes into smaller apartments. The largest ones had split the houses four ways, one unit for each floor. These each featured a small business or two on the bottom floor, a half story below street level. I'd spotted bookstores, clothing boutiques, bars, and more on our way in.

Across the street, at number 358, was a coffee shop and right next to it, an art gallery. I fought the urge to go get a cup while Hargold worked through whatever was bothering him.

Even with the more spacious dwellings mixed in most of the buildings were now eight separate dwellings. These were split by floor, as well as the right and left halves of the building. The basement of each of the structures was almost invariably given over to the equipment needed to run it as well as a laundry. Some had an apartment for a manager, others a storefront, and the rest offered private storage for each tenant.

The most cramped were just like number 357; meant for singletons or students attending one of the colleges of the nearby universities. These sixteen—plus one for the manager—apartment buildings were short on space, but still remained desirable. Seaward was a good section of New Dagonia. The apartments had access to the shops dotting the neighborhood. On top of that, the ward's watchtower was well-funded.

As such, the small apartments were popular enough to nearly always be full. But not so popular that their prices became unreasonable. Even so, Seaward's unique architecture had been a regular stop on our hit list for six years. Middle-class bliss and student life both ended all too often in tears.

And blood.

After a couple of minutes' silence Thief finally spoke. "Let me take the lead." I nodded, expecting him to get out of the carry. But he paused another full minute before whatever imperceptible cue he was waiting for spurred him to action.

I climbed out of the Hallowstone right after Hargold. We walked past the cordon, flashing our sigils to the uniform. A brisk couple of steps up the half-flight which lay before the building led us up into the divided row house's lobby. We passed through a door with the kind of lock that was common forty years ago, before the proliferation of jigglers, which held charge enough to pop a few simple locks before being drained.

A set of seventeen small mail boxes were set on the wall at the base of the central stairway.

"Poor security," I said as we started up the steps. "That's par for the course on lower rent buildings, of course, but whoever came in wouldn't have been slowed down much by that door."

Thief nodded, and we wound our way up to the fourth floor. The haste evident in my partner as we'd mounted the steps out front had retreated. Each flight was slower than the last, and I wondered at his return to silence following the order to let him lead. I dropped back as we neared the top of the building and followed him in silence.

At the top of the stairs he paused and turned to me. I saw him wanting to speak, but his mouth snapped shut and he shifted to look at apartment 4D.

The open door was sturdy, if in need of a paint job. A solid new double lock was set in the portal, and like the front entrance the doorway had been cordoned off. A uniform was visible inside, writing on a notepad. His position marked him as the officer controlling access to the apartment. Another scene like the hundreds we'd visited together.

Only this time Thief remained frozen in place, staring at the open portal. A minute passed before I heard him suck in a deep breath.

I expected him to step in. But something odd happened instead.

My completely irreligious partner knelt and made a sign of devotion to Akala, the goddess of dark places.

I was still recovering from the shock of the gesture when Hargold ducked the cordon and made his way inside.

When I managed to get over my surprise, I caught up to Thief in the living area of the apartment. He was looking down at the body of our victim, a once dark-haired—but now graying—

middle-aged man. Three holes had been put in him; two in the chest, one in the head. The third hole was situated just above his sad, brown eyes.

My first thought was that the wounds were about what an ice wand—but not a powerful one—would leave. The holes were small, but even. I looked around and spotted a bagged-up wand lying near my feet, next to the shelving built into the wall.

"Hey handsome," said a voice behind me. I turned to see Mari Umren, one of the newer necromancers. She had her hair up—as usual—and was wearing her ever-present spectacles. The whole look is conservative, but sassy. Like a naughty librarian, or the tutor I'd had during my first year at university.

Mari and I flirt for fun whenever we run into each other over a dead body. Sometimes I wonder if there's more than casual flirtation there, but I don't have a lot of time for relationships, and she's never made a real move.

"Hello yourself, beautiful." I said. I stepped aside and let her into the living area. "How'd you luck out and get a day shift?"

"Oh yeah, lucky me." She sighed and shook her head. "I'm pulling a double. I should be off and enjoying three whole days of relaxation with friends at the boardwalk."

"Ouch. Hope they catch the bastard." I shot her a sympathetic half smile. "Were you headed to Taniston?"

"It's Greene. He's sick again." She set her case on the floor and started to unload it. "And no, we were going to Yarlow. My friends are headed out of town at this very second, and I've got to make my own way. I'm missing the Aimie Slayte show tonight. I can feel it."

I nodded. Slayte was a hot ticket, and even a recluse like me knew it. A midweek trip to one of the boardwalk resort towns in nearby Amilar might not have the excitement of a weekend, but quality attractions like shows from some of the hottest acts in the Thousand Kingdoms were available any day of the week.

I pointed at the victim. "What's up with our body?"

"I just got here, but it looks to me like he took an ice wand at close range. Probably chest first."

"The third is from above when he was already down," said the DMU detective down the hallway.

"I'll need to get him to the Slabs to verify that, but it wouldn't surprise me if that's the order."

"Execution," said Thief.

"Looks like it, yes." Mari leaned around me and smiled up at my partner. "Morning Hargold. Didn't think I'd see you boys out."

He grunted. Then something oddly poetic crossed his lips. "Well, Murder, it's come to this."

"It usually does," she said, tilting her head. "You ok?"

"Yeah. His name. It's Murder."

"What?" I asked, but then it hit me. "Hold on, his name is actually Murder?"

"His name is Gallan Armos," said the uniform by the door. "Neighbor who found him gave us the ID when we got here."

"The one he took when they let him, yeah," Thief said as he circled the body. Mari and I shuffled slightly to let him pass through the cramped space. "He was less inclined than I was to embrace the legacy his mother left him."

New Dagonia's history was colorful. My partner's particular experiences were part of that tradition.

For centuries prisoners who gave birth in the higher security New Dagonian institutions were forced to have their children's surnames legally documented as some variation of the crime the woman had committed. Each convict was presented with a short list of surnames her child could be given. Usually the prisoners had been granted no more than half an hour to choose once asked. Failure to decide resulted in a name being chosen for the infant.

Children born—and subsequently raised—in the prisons were given surnames such as Arson, Robber, Rabblerouser, and Whore; among others. So Thief was branded by his mother's transgressions from birth. The law was abolished two decades ago, and individuals with such names were subsequently allowed to legally change them. Many took their mother's original name back. Others were finally allowed to adopt their spouse's surname.

Thief hadn't bothered, and in a way his decision had made me feel more at ease with him. My own name wasn't handed down from my parents, or chosen by anything more reliable than the ramblings of a fortunetelling witch. That bond made us kindred spirits in a way.

My curiosity was aroused by the name, and I had to ask. "Did you meet him when...you—"

Hargold cut the question off. "Yeah." He nodded slowly. "Funny to say after so long, but he was my best friend back then. We grew up together."

"I'm sorry, Hargold," said Mari in a soft voice.

"Don't be. We went different ways."

"How'd you know he lived here then?" I asked.

He turned away from Gallan Armos'—or, Murder's—corpse and widened his eyes. "Well, that's the interesting part...."

CHAPTER 3

Thief was born during his mother's decade long stint in a high security prison and workhouse named Greenfields Reformatory. The place was shut down before I was born, back when the Council abolished sentences for the children of inmates. Facilities like Greenfields dried up or were converted into institutions which would better serve strictly adult populations.

When her baby boy was born, Moira Callae was given five choices for his surname: Thief, Assaulter, Stealer, Steal, and Bitch.

The last option was an attempt at torture by the guards; but Hargold's mother had been a tough woman, and not easy prey. In fact, her reputation as a fighter meant he'd had as good an upbringing as a child could have inside Greenfields. He'd gotten a fair share of food, and not been subjected to abuse by the other children. Moira's boy became strictly off limits after a disfiguring accident befell a woman whose son—older than Thief by several months—had pushed the toddler down during their afternoon play time.

Still, from the time he was six until he was released with his mother at nine, Hargold worked six days a week. He and the other boys were tasked with the labor-intensive—and disgusting—tanning process, while the women and girls handled all kinds of leatherwork.

All of this I knew already. What I didn't know is how he'd met our victim. So, I found myself enthralled as he began to narrate this fresh episode from his past.

"Gallan and I were friends before I could even talk right," he said. "His mom and mine were a lot alike. Both respected—or feared, if I'm honest—and influential. They could have been enemies, but I guess something when they met told them they'd make better friends, so they chose that road instead."

He pointed at his old friend's body. "They called us 'darkness and light' for our hair. We pretty much ruled the roost together. None of the other children ever dared cross us. We were nobility." He shook his head. "The kind of nobility that ruled with violence and fear; proper nobles from before the Age of Enlightenment."

Thief ticked off fingers for a moment, then continued. "We were inseparable until I was eight. I remember because I could count the rest of my mom's term in months. Gallan was a couple years older, but he was in until sixteen because his mother's sentence was thirty years. He wasn't named Murder for nothing."

He frowned. "He beat me out of Greenfields though. One morning they found his mother dead. He was carted off to the cemetery, had a look at her body as they tossed it in the ground, and was packed off the same morning. They gave him just enough time to grab his possessions and threw him out into the arms of an orphanage."

A shiver went up my spine at the mention of the institution. I knew that Murder had been in prison before the orphanage, but if Greenfields had been his home, he was likely just as scared as I'd been when they'd taken me away.

"Six years later my mother and I were out of the prison. I'd taken on an apprenticeship with a leatherworker who enjoyed my mother's company—and her bed—and was well on my way to becoming mediocre at the trade. My daily job was to handle the rough work in the yard out back, and my mother's was to deal with customers."

He shrugged. "I saw him by accident, really. My mother was ill and I'd taken her place in the front. I heard shouting and checked outside. Running flat out was this fool. People were shouting 'police' and 'pickpocket' behind him."

Thief ducked his head and turned slightly red. "It wasn't wise, but I'd like to think it was at least noble to have maintained my loyalty to him. Even after so many years. I my oldest friend him until the uniforms were well away. For my troubles Murder stole a pair of boots right out of the shop, and I got a hiding from my mother."

He paused for a few moments and stared down at his friend. Nobody so much as shifted. We all just stared at him, waiting for the rest.

"Seems like a couple of lifetimes later we ran across each other again. It was in court. But not because he was in trouble again. He'd gone legitimate. Changed his name. I hadn't even realized who he was; my partner had interviewed him. But one day there he stood, right in the middle of one of my homicide trials."

"The man had changed. Stood up and testified that he'd seen our killer go into the back of a bar called the Lizard's Gizzard one night after a gig. Two minutes later the same man came out chasing the joint's barman with a bloody knife."

Hargold's voice got quiet. "Gallan ran away. But he didn't do it to save his own skin—or, well, he did kind of—but no, what I mean is he ran and he got help. After that, he went to trial. Even though the guy was pretty bad news, and had a lot of friends. Then he put the bastard away."

Mari put her hand on his shoulder. "Oh Hargold, maybe you didn't go such different ways after all."

"I know a man can change, but I'd never really understood what it meant until I saw him up in front of the magistrates that day. Whenever I think of the word 'redemption' now, it's Murder's face I see. Mostly though, I figured that we'd probably never see each other again. And honestly, I didn't think of him much at all."

He stared down at the corpse of his friend, then tipped his head and right shoulder in a half-shrug. "I guess I was wrong."

"But you knew this was his address?" I asked.

"Last week I got a chime from Gallan. He wanted to talk to me." He paused and shook his head hard, sending blond hair flying. No, he was desperate to talk to me, really. He begged me to come meet him today after work."

"What for?" I asked.

"Fuck if I know, and now he's dead." Hargold Thief does not cry. But I swear—for just a second—I saw his eyes well up. He turned and walked over to a small table which contained Armos' clarion, a stack of mail, and a pad of paper.

"He didn't say more than that? Why today?"

"Because of the out of town gigs. I don't mean like playing in the enclaves. He was damned good, apparently. He wasn't even in New Dagonia when he called. I'm not sure where he'd been on tour, but he called me from Sallee."

"When did he get in?"

"When we talked, Gallan said he'd be coming in late on Sunday. That's why I told him I'd make time tonight. He got that I was going to head over here after work, and that I'd try to be early. He wasn't happy about having to wait though."

"I can see why."

"Do you think I don't fucking know that?" Thief roared as he rounded on me and took a step across the intervening space. I froze. I'm taller, but I wouldn't put money on myself if it came to a brawl. He out-masses me by a fair bit, and it's still mostly muscle. Plus, he's the meanest bastard I've ever met.

"Hargold, he didn't mean it that way," said Mari.

I shook my head. "I'm not blaming you, brother," I said.

"I know...but I am." He turned back to the table and picked up the mail. I let him be, and put some space between us.

I headed out to the hallway, where I reached out to dispatch and asked for a check on the man's passport. I suspected he really had come into the aerodrome on Sunday night, but it was worth verifying. The answer came back within minutes. He'd come in from Sallee, and landed at 8:23PM.

A quick chat with the uniform turned up the basics of how the call had been initiated. The woman who'd chimed emergency services lived in 4C. She'd heard what sounded like dog barking, and three loud, sharp noises. Immediately afterward she ran out of her flat to investigate.

Someone—a man she'd described as dark-haired, not young, and slightly scarred—had run out of Gallan's apartment and slid down the stairs, leaving the door open. When she'd looked inside, Armos had been dead; lying sprawled out on the floor next to the wand that killed him. At just after 8:30AM she'd chimed to report the crime.

The depressing irony of his demise hit me at that moment. Murder had been murdered.

I didn't share my thought with Thief.

CHAPTER 4

Tuesday's scene in the bull pen was subdued. The entire third floor was on eggshells, owing mainly to what had happened upon our return to Hammersmith on Monday afternoon.

Hovering over Mari at the Crypt hadn't produced anything useful, and Hargold's mood had been delicate by the time we'd arrived back at the watchtower. Falcon's ill-timed decision to ask the 'loser' how the scene had been had not gone over well.

Monday's coffeepot throwing demonstration had solidified my partner's reputation as both extremely coordinated and wildly unpredictable. Fortunately for Bird, cops have good medical coverage.

And thick skulls.

So by the time Tuesday rolled around everyone was ready to steer well clear of Thief. Things were even more hushed than I'd come to expect after a blowout between the two because Rabino was skipping out on roll call. Dispatch had sent him off to handle a robbery gone bad in Archstone.

I'd cursed myself for not checking in on the way in, because the call would have been mine if I'd just gone with my routine. But after Monday's string of unpleasant events I'd wanted the extra time knowing I was safe from any calls. It wasn't until I was headed up into the bull pen that I'd reported for duty, and by then Rabbit was already on scene, just a dozen blocks from my loft.

All of which added up to me being the one who'd gotten stuck babysitting a heavily-bandaged Bird and an angry lion.

My squadmates were primarily occupied with glowering at each other as the seconds ticked down to 9:00AM.

Hargold spent the time he wasn't giving Kif dirty looks leafing through pages of mug shots and sketches. We hoped for some kind of a match to the sketch the art specialist had produced based on the witness' description of the man she'd spotted fleeing the scene. But with dozens of books down we hadn't even come close to finding a suspect that fit.

"Ow," said Falcon, about every minute or two. This served to irritate Thief further, and made me consider heading to the armory to pick up a lighting rod.

Just in case they got frisky.

We shuffled out of our domain at the usual time; a minute to the hour. I sent Bird up the steps and pushed my partner into the lift. They glared at each other until losing eye contact. I couldn't help the sigh which escaped my lips. It got me some looks from the Robbery Unit detectives who we shared the ride with, but I knew they understood.

The lift dumped Hargold and me, along with a load of other detectives collected from the fourth and fifth, out on the sixth floor just a minute later. Kif was already sitting in Homicide Unit's corner of the assembly area. He looked a little winded, but at least it proved he was well enough to jog a few flights just to irk Thief.

He'd taken my partner's normal seat.

"Leave it," I said as we approached. I got a grunt in return, so I grabbed his thick arm and held him back for a moment. "I mean it, Hargold." He nodded and I didn't spot any defiance in his icy eyes.

We took our seats and the three of us waited for the official start time of 9:05AM to come around. Falcon didn't end up with more stitches, which I was willing to count as a victory.

Detective Lieutenant Saund started roll call in the sixth floor assembly area with Robbery Unit's cases. One of their detectives was off with Rabino, but the other three spent a few minutes reporting progress on primeshift's open cases.

Saund worked through the pending issues facing each of the specialist squads in a precise, detailed manner. The DLt ran a tight breakdown every day, but she was extra vigilant in crushing chatter during this particular meeting.

Strangely, she didn't actually run down our unit's open cases. That was a first for me. In six years on HU, roll call had always included a status update from my squad, even when we didn't have any cases with new activity.

As the gathering broke apart she asked us—by name—to hang back. That request, coupled with the lack of update from us, got the three of us looks from the other detectives. Fortunately, after the ball-crushing intolerance Saund had shown throughout the morning's proceedings, we weren't subjected to any ribbing. I knew it was just a temporary reprieve. Even with Hargold's outburst fresh in their minds, passing up the chance to zing another unit simply wasn't done.

"Captain wants a word," she said when it was just the four of us. "I'll walk with."

We filed out and headed to Trawler's office back on the third floor. We took the stairs; Saund kept pace next to me, between Thief and Falcon. I flashed her a grateful look. She shrugged and gave me an eyeroll.

The Captain rated the penthouse spread up on the thirteenth floor, of course. But when the hard-nosed dwarf had taken control of the watchtower three years earlier he'd decided to do things differently. On his orders half of the third floor records area was cleared out, and he'd set up shop between the pens for Homicide and Robbery.

Aside from making a few of the older detectives uncomfortable with the loss of some of the less valuable hard copy archives to storage at Timberhold, the arrangement had worked well. Trawler's affinity for the two squads showed, and our closure rate had actually improved with his guidance. It wasn't a night and day change, but it had made him popular at central without costing him morale at home.

The four of us filed into the office. With only a pair of seats available in front of the desk none of us moved to sit down. Saund took a position to the side of the massive bureau and leaned against the shelf. That left my squadmates and me to array ourselves in front.

Captain Argo Trawler pointedly ignored us. He was busy scrawling his signature onto a stack of paperwork.

Sign. Flip. Sign. Flip.

Trawler was big for a dwarf. He was nearly five feet tall, which made him the second largest dwarven cop I'd ever met. He was well-muscled, like most of his folk, and at his age—all of sixty three—still in his prime.

A twenty-eight year veteran of the force, Trawler had joined up the day he was eligible. And he'd no doubt go on to serve as long as they'd let him. For most of his kin mandatory retirement was a hundred, but I knew there had been a notable exception or two that managed a couple of decades longer. He oozed cop from every pore, and that had no doubt helped him make Captain.

"You boys are a pain in my ass." Trawler finished signing the last of the pile and tossed his stylus on the desk. "Thief, I'm sure Falcon was being a prick," he said as he stared Kif down, "but you broke a coffee set, and my detectives need coffee to close cases. More importantly, I need coffee to deal with you idiots." The dwarf paused for a moment, then nodded at me. "These two dummies going to kill each other, Dire?"

I let my eyes slide sideways. "Kill...might be harsh, Captain."

He grunted. "Can you please do me a favor, Hargold?" My partner just glowered, so Trawler shrugged. "I'm going to take that as a 'yes' because I can." He jabbed a thick, stubby finger at Falcon. "Leave Bird alone and hold your shit together. You've got four days to go. Don't lose it now."

Thief's brow smashed together and he took a half step forward. "Captain, I—"

Trawler cut him off with a sharp gesture. "No. Detective Sergeant, you have a case to work on. Stay out of the watchtower as much as you can while you do it. Go short-time it on the streets."

"Yes, Captain," he said.

"Now, Dire?"

I leaned in slightly. "Aye, Captain?"

"I can make your life miserable if he causes any more trouble."

"Aye, Captain." The bastard would, at that.

"Bird?"

"Captain," said Falcon.

"Next time duck." Kif turned red but didn't respond. Trawler picked his stylus up and started to shuffle through a fresh pile of reports. "All of you, get lost. Close some cases."

CHAPTER 5

Wednesday was a better day.

Of course that might have had something to do with the fact that it couldn't have been worse than Tuesday. We'd left Hammersmith only to chase down leads generated by running all of Murder's known criminal associates for a couple of hours.

But that afternoon—which then led into the evening, and on into the night—produced nothing more than a dozen dead ends. That was, in and of itself, less than thrilling.

Nothing we hadn't dealt with in the past, of course, but Thief had been determined to prove himself the highlight of the experience. He'd done his level best to demonstrate what a foul mood he was in at every turn. The whole time we'd been on the streets I had felt more like a nanny than a partner. I'd even dragged him away from more than one line of inquiry before he started a fight.

By the time we'd knocked off it had been closing in on midnight, and I'd been ready to keel over from exhaustion. All that work had been capped off with a single drink—with no time for real relaxation—before we'd crashed at Hargold's place.

Wednesday morning had dawned clear, and bright. Thief had taken the time to buy me breakfast at the local diner and apologize for Tuesday's behavior before we'd headed off to see if we could drum up any more leads.

Any day that starts with bacon has got good chances.

The brilliant suggestion I'd made as we'd gotten started had been to check with Gallan's places of employment. In theory it sounded great. Having exhausted the crooks he'd associated with in the distant past on Tuesday—or at least the ones that were still breathing and on the streets—I figured it was time to treat his killing as if a respectable, successful musician had been killed.

After all, for two decades that's what he'd been.

In practice, things proved more difficult than I'd hoped. Murder—as my partner called him every time we were alone—had worked gigs almost every bar or club in the entire city-state. That was daunting enough, so we confined ourselves to the haunts he played most regularly.

The twenty places we hit before collapsing at Hargold's just before two in the morning were each a bust. Nobody had a single ill word to say about Gallan Armos. Everyone we'd talked to had reacted with appropriate amounts of shock and dismay.

So, when I hold Wednesday up as an example of a 'better' day, I suppose I just mean that breakfast was free.

Thursday just made me long for breakfast, even if I had to pay for it. Thief kicked me off his couch at 4:56AM. I made my way into the kitchen to find something resembling coffee, but the foray was short-lived. I hadn't managed to open a single cabinet before my partner grabbed me by the back of my wrinkled shirt and dragged me out onto the streets.

We were at Hammersmith by 5:28AM. Our first order of business was starting a dig through cases colder than glacial runoff. Hargold wanted to know if there was anything unsolved which connected to Murder's life via his close associates from the time before he went straight. Even a tiny connection.

That meant the eyestrain of checking all of Gallan's 'friends' for involvement in the cases stored in the historical section. There was still only one way to do that, even with the new archival devices central had started rolling out. The HCU records weren't due for transfer until next year. Which meant the only way to get what we needed was through a physical search of the unit's archives.

The process reminded me that one of my deepest fears was that some day very soon the NDPD would need a lone second class to fill a slot in the Historical Crimes Unit. Being relegated to squinting at ancient offenses in the dim, eighth floor office of the HCU was the stuff of my nightmares. Even if all the cases were at least serious in nature, the closure rate in the unit was abysmal.

The one redeeming factor of Detective Fartower's bailiwick was that his squad had their own private break area—complete with coffee maker—buried in the middle of their work area. I guessed from the scattered files that it might not even be a break area. It looked as if the team spent most of their working hours in the central section as well.

I imagined they'd need to snort coffee grounds just to stay awake.

By 8:30AM Fartower and two other detectives had shown up to get started. They greeted us and made a few inquiries about what we were looking for, but otherwise left us to it. None of them seemed overly concerned or interested in what we were up to. If anything, Fartower seemed bored by us.

Just before 9:00AM I was ready to violate the spirit of Captain Trawler's edict banning us from associating with the other detectives. I was willing to risk the dwarf's wrath by dragging Thief down to roll call just to be doing anything but checking a stack of robbery reports no more recent than twenty years in the past.

The escape plans were put on hold as a sketch in one of the dozens of folders I was working with caught my eye. A dark-haired young man stared out at me from the page. He was a fair bit younger and certainly more intact than the corpse I'd seen on Monday, but I was gazing into the sad eyes of Gallan Armos, back when he still was named Murder.

"Hargold," I said.

"No, we're not going to get some food, and Trawler will kill us if we go to roll call. Read your damned files."

My stomach growled in protest, but I pressed on. "Look over here you numpty." He glanced up from his own pile and leapt out of his seat to grab the sketch.

"Yes!"

"Armed robbery at a storage facility with three suspects," I said, reading from the reports. "Happened twenty five years ago. Witnesses provided a sketch for Gallan, but he was never picked up." I flipped the page and skimmed it before continuing. "There was never an actual ID connected with the picture, either. Which doesn't surprise me, considering how clean he actually kept himself. He was no dummy."

"But that's him."

I nodded. I'd never met Murder in his prime, but the eyes were a giveaway. "One of the other perps was killed trying to escape, after he fired on the officers responding to the call. He was foreign, or at least no New Dagonian record of him was found, so he was buried nameless after Necro got done with him."

"Anything on the third?"

"The only thing the police have from the witnesses is a name that was shouted. The downed man kept calling for a man named 'Taand' before he bled out. Nobody by that name was ever turned up with any kind of connection. I've got a short list of people with the last name Taand in the city at the time, and each is noted as having no known criminal connections or activity."

"Wait, you're saying 'tand' is something the guy repeated."

"T-A-A-N-D, is what they wrote down. Report reads that the subject kept repeating 'Taand...' and 'man...' until he expired."

"That might not be a name. Not a person's name at least." He pulled out a notepad and flipped through it, then circled something. "Here." He held the pad out to me and I took it.

"Tandem Holdings," I said. "What's that?"

"A return address in the stack of letters at Gallan's apartment. That one was the kind of letter you get when someone sends you a cheque. Right weight of paper for it, and a piece of the letter was missing at the bottom. Letter itself was a bunch of meaningless words, like whoever sent it had nothing to say, but did anyway."

"How does that connect?"

"I dunno. Keep digging in the file?"

I flipped through the pages, skimming the reports. They were fairly slim so it only took a couple of minutes before I found something. "Take a look at this." I handed the folder over.

"What?" Thief read the page and shook his head. "You're kidding. He stole property described as 'valuable trade secrets' from Tandem Holdings?"

I took the file back as he offered it. "Aye. So why would he steal from a company, then get money from that very same company decades later?"

Thief sighed. "The better question might be what idiot's name is on the case?"

"Uh, Detective Sergeant Jam—"

"Jamlan!"

"Yeah."

"Asshole."

"You knew him?"

Thief shook his head. "I knew of him. He got kicked out after making primeshift lead in Robbery Unit and deciding that he was done working hard. Closure rate in the unit went to shit and they canned him."

I winced. "Ouch. For the unit, not him."

"Was a huge deal at the time because he fought the department's action. My Sergeant spent every day at roll call during the scandal making it clear that, unlike Jamlan, patrol officers actually worked for a living."

"Huh. So Gallan gets away to start a new life because of a lazy cop." I shook my head. "What a break for him."

"Break for us too. That Tandem connection is too strange to be ignored." Thief rubbed his beard for a moment then tilted his head. "Gallan is in a crew that forces their way into a storage facility. He steals from a specific company. Yet he gets mail from that company years later?" His brow wrinkled. "What does that add up to?"

I thought about it for a moment. "Honestly? I have no idea. But you're right, it's way too weird to ignore."

We stared at each other for a long while after that. Finally Thief stood up and grabbed his trench coat. "Well, if all we have to go on is Tandem, we may as well go to the source for our info."

"We're going to go knock on their doors?"

"Not that source. We're headed to Timberhold. To the FCD." He walked away, humming an old melody.

I grabbed my duster and fedora as I followed. Just before I walked out of HCU Fartower smiled at me. "Nice find, Detective. You've got a talent for historical work."

"Thanks." As I scurried out of the unit I could have sworn his expression was downright predatory. I shook myself and called to my partner. "Wait up!"

I couldn't get on the lift fast enough.

One of the specialty sections not housed at Hammersmith is the Financial Crimes Division. They handle all of the embezzlement, tax evasion, fraud, and similar non-violent, money-oriented crimes. They deal in a whole lot of fines and penalties, and less actual arrests and trials than most of the NDPD. Much of what they handle is civil, not criminal. That said, every FCD detective still carries a wand.

Thief and I were in the lobby of the division by 10:29AM. We'd called ahead, but the Detective Lieutenant we were slated to meet with had gotten into one of those meetings you can't seem to escape from. The receptionist—an actual civilian, and not an unattractive one—apologized for DLt Canner's tardiness, and offered us more coffee as we waited.

It wasn't until 10:53AM that we were finally escorted to the lift and sent up to the seventh floor. As we waited for the stop and go at every floor, I got a good look at my partner for the first time since Monday.

To say he looked rough would have been an insult to the word. Thief's normally bushy hair had gone flat. There were bags under the bags under his eyes; I wondered if he'd slept at all while I had been crashed on his couch. But the most disturbing part of his visage was that his naturally squared, beefy face looked gaunt.

The doors to the lift slid open on seven. We stepped out behind a pair of detectives who'd boarded on the third. A stern, gray-haired woman nodded to us as we looked around the small lobby area. She wasn't unattractive, but I figured she was probably older than my partner. "Detectives," she said, nodding to us. "I'm, Detective Lieutenant Canner, interim head of the Fraud Squad."

"Interim?" I asked as she motioned for us to follow her.

"Our Captain retired," she said as she led us down the hallway. "I'm actually the lead for one of our teams. I run ITI. That's Insider Trading Investigations."

"You need to be a Captain just to head the Fraud Squad?" I asked as we turned a corner. "That's just one part of FCD though, right?"

"Our division is run by a Deputy Inspector, actually. The Captain reports to the Commander who serves as a coordinator and filter. Only the most important stuff goes all the way up."

"How many detectives work here?"

"Four hundred twenty or so," she said.

I tripped over my own feet. "Four—"

"I know it seems like a lot, Detective, but we handle the entire nation's financial, insurance, and corporate crimes." She shook her head. "Billions of liri are lost every year to non-violent financial crimes. In New Dagonia people get killed in business a lot more often than on the streets."

"It's a lot less permanent." Thief's voice was low, dangerous. I punched his arm and he glared at me. Canner turned. "But very important," he said in a voice so full of false cheer that I cringed.

I held up my hands. "The case is personal." Thief grunted.

Canner nodded and gestured for us to follow her down a side passage. "Believe it or not, I was a patrol officer once. I have a distant memory of the streets."

"We know," I said. I gave her a winning smile. She gave me a look up and down. Thief just sighed. I couldn't see him, but I'm sure he was rolling his eyes.

"I've had someone set out everything we have, but I can't spare any time to help you right now." She opened up a door and waved us through. "You should be comfortable in here while you look over the Tandem Holdings records. Sorry that it's still in hard copy. We're not slated for full archival for another four years. We have more paper than any other division, too." She sighed. "You can feel free to use any of our facilities. Make yourselves at home." Canner checked the chrono hanging on the far wall of the room. "Now, I have to run. Banking fraud briefing in five."

"Thank you," I said as Thief shuffled in.

"My pleasure, Detective." Canner leaned in. "If you're ever thirsty...," she said in a low voice. I felt her press a card into my hand and I pocketed it. I smiled pleasantly at her as she left. The door clicked and I let out the sigh I'd been holding in.

If I was going to hang around with middle-aged cops and drink I preferred it be with Thief. The card came out of my pocket and went in the bin. "You have to antagonize her? Some of us still work next week."

"Fucking pencil-pushing desk jockey. 'Killed in business' my ass."

"Let's see if the desk jockey has anything useful for us before you judge her too harshly?"

"Oh she has something all right. Your favorite." He waved his hand at a stack of old files on the desk. "Dig in, Griff."

Suddenly I wanted it to be Tuesday again.

☆   ☆   ☆
☆   ☆   ☆

"What's this shit?" asked my partner as he walked back in to find me face down, half asleep in the middle of a pile of files.

I groaned. "This is me dying. Tell them I was killed by OT. Also, confess to having wielded that weapon with malice while you're at it. You belong back in prison, sadist."

"Shut up and eat something." He tossed me a bag and sat down. I opened the sack; the smell of charred meat assaulted my nostrils. My mouth flooded with saliva.

"Oh thank you, there is mercy in this cruel world." I jerked a kebab out of the bag and tore into it. I made extra noise with my lips and chewed more loudly than was strictly necessary in an effort to show my appreciation.

Thief just shook his head. "Did you find anything while I was out, or just sleep?"

I tried to talk, failed, chewed some more, and swallowed. "When the theft happened it was reported, and insurance paid out."

"That's so four hours ago of you, Dire."

"Right," I said. "So we think insurance fraud."

"And waste hours on that."

"Exactly." I nod. "It wasn't fraud. The payment was pathetic because the item stolen had very little proven value."

"I know." He shrugged. "I was the one who said 'trade secrets' weren't worth anything."

"So if it wasn't fraud, 'what was it,' I asked myself."

"Did you beat around the bush this much when you talked it over with yourself?"

"Yes," I said and took a bite of my kebab.

Thief growled.

"Fine," I said, chewing the meat carefully in the side of my mouth. "Nothing leads back to insurance fraud," I yawned for effect. He grinned. "But we have this connection to a foreigner who died at the scene."

"So?"

"Right after Tandem lost whatever was in that unit they had a change of ownership."

"Huh?" Thief reached for the file in front of me and started to flip through it.

I downed the bite and went for another one as he read. The wait for chow had been a long one, but there were no finer sticks of meat than the beauties sold by Jaq's in Dawn Gate. Hargold had refused to run for them until after the rush, but if you had to wait until after eight to eat, you wanted to have something amazing.

Jaq's kebabs more than qualified.

"Well damn," Thief said as he set the file down, "you should transfer over here after I leave. Save you fighting off Fartower's advances."

"I hope you get shot tomorrow," I said in an icy tone.

He grinned. "Seriously, I couldn't have found that."

"So, remember that we checked Tandem for any anomalies financially, and there were none. That seemed very strange to me, because everyone has ups and downs, right? The markets run on that."

"I'm going to have Detective Lieutenant Cougar request you."

"I will shoot you myself, brother." I raised my arm and wiggled it at him. I left the wand in its wrist sheath.

For the moment.

"So it was too steady?" he asked.

"By far. Money in, money out, money in, money out. Like clockwork."

He sunk back into the chair. "Laundering."

"Laundering," I said.

"So we've got what looks a lot like a hostile takeover of a laundering front, but how?"

"Extortion using whatever was in storage, probably. Seems like the most likely thing the 'trade secrets' were. Compromising documents." I shook my head. "Honestly, I don't know if we've got enough to go on to figure that out. Besides, we already have a case."

"Murder."

"So what if the letter from Tandem isn't what set him off? What if he always gets letters from them. Say, with money?"

Thief held up a finger. "We've got to check—"

"His financials," I said. "Rabino was still at the watchtower, he ran them while I was getting information on Tandem from OCU."

"And?"

"Every month. Added up to somewhere near eight or nine

thousand liri a year, and got a bit bigger in the middle of each year that passed."

"For the whole time?"

"Rabbit couldn't check past five years quickly, but it held true."

Thief grunted and rubbed his face with both hands. He looked ten years older than usual. "I thought he was straight."

"Maybe he needed that score to get right. Though from what Rabbit said he seemed to be doing fine. He didn't need it recently. Died with a couple hundred thousand liri in the bank."

"You're not on the level if you're taking a payoff," he said, but he seemed unconvinced. "What'd OCU say?"

"Tandem holds the papers for a bunch of street level businesses. Mostly Kaid's Cross and the Black Spit."

"Not—"

"No, no," I said. "Nothing on the spit. Not actually inside the Warrens. Just normal stuff. But—"

"Seaward!" Thief slammed his fists into the table.

"Yes. In fact, they own the entire block he lives in."

"I bet he never paid rent," said Thief.

"I doubt that. Rabino didn't see anything out of the ordinary, and he's not an idiot. Missing rent would have looked wrong to him."

"Rabbit go home?"

"Normal people do. Even detectives." I tapped the notes I'd made. "He wouldn't have missed that. You know how he is."

"Fine. What do we have on Tandem physically?"

"Nothing. Some papers got changed around after the heist, but they don't really exist. OCU has the company in a file of interesting businesses, but there's no actual leads. They've got no traction on who runs it, and they have bigger problems than a laundry."

"Murder was getting paid by them, so they have to exist."

I nodded. "He was, and they do exist on paper and in bank accounts. In fact they're not much more than money in bank accounts. Beyond that the company's address has always been linked to a secure mail facility."

"Where?"

"First in Kaid's Cross, and then Heartcore after the change of ownership. Which, I might add, I only think was a change in ownership. Probably." I shrugged. "Could have just as easily been an inheritance or a shift in management is what I mean."

"But why the center of the city?" asked Thief as he rubbed his temples. "These fronts are all in low rent areas. Except for part of Seaward, I suppose."

"If I had to guess, I'd say it was more convenient for whoever is in control," I said.

"For whoever took over."

I shrugged. "Seems likely, but we can't be sure. I can't think of any other reason to move the damned address than being too lazy to go all the way to Kaid's Cross to get your mail."

Hargold sighed. "What is this mess? Murder was killed for something. My gut is screaming at me that Tandem, and whoever is behind the company, is too shady to ignore."

"I have no idea what's going on, brother." I popped the last bite of my stick into my mouth. "But I do know that these kebabs were worth the wait."

"Eat up, you're going to need your strength."

The look in his eyes made me want to cry. I settled for digging into the sack for another spicy skewer and enjoying my dinner.

CHAPTER 7

Friday didn't start the way I'd thought it would.

In the version I had imagined, I would have picked Hargold up and taken him into the office by way of his favorite diner. We would have shared a leisurely breakfast with some genuine laughs. I'd figured it would be sad, but heart-warming.

What I got was coffee slapped on the table and a rough shake to get me up off Hargold's couch. "Get up," he said in a voice that sounded like thunder to my sleepy ears. "We've got work to do."

"Mmm...get shot...," I mumbled, and reached for the coffee.

Ten minutes—and all the coffee—later I was awake enough to check my chrono. 4:53AM coalesced above my palm. "What the fuck, Hargold? Three hours of sleep? I'm going to shoot you myself."

"Save your piss and vinegar for someone who deserves it," he said as he walked into the room. "Have a look at the warrant."

"What war—" I stopped as I spotted the paper on the table. I flipped it open and read through it. "How...it's the middle of the night."

"I don't need my favors any more after today, do I?" He said it quietly. I looked across the living area to where he stood, sipping his own cup. He was leaning on the counter. I wondered if he'd fall over without the support.

"You didn't sleep at all, did you?"

"I can sleep for the rest of my life."

"You look worse than awful. You know that, right?"

"Thanks Griff, I try." I was struck by the fact that he sounded as bad as he looked.

For a moment I was tempted to get on the link to dispatch and have them drag Trawler out of bed to shut Thief down. But the hardened veteran who'd brought me into the life was right there, not ten feet away, looking at me with his damnably intense ice blue eyes. Without saying a word he was begging me to do what we had to do to catch one last killer.

I sighed, yawned, and thrust myself upright. "So, what're we waiting for?" I asked as I headed for the door to collect my duster and fedora.

As I walked past my partner I saw a tiny, weary smile.

Never mind how it started, Friday also didn't play out even close to the way I'd imagined.

Somewhere along the line I'd picked up this idea that once we got to work we'd be greeted by a morning filled with war stories, cutting jokes, and maybe some nice pastries. Colleagues from every floor of the watchtower would come by to pay their respects, maybe.

That would have been so nice.

As it was, when we'd hit the streets I remembered—with an appropriate helping of regret—wishing for one last case on Monday. The world is a twisted place sometimes.

So, with a case on our plate and a single day to handle it in, we'd commandeered two patrol units as escorts before it was even a quarter past five. Doubtless more favors I hadn't known Thief had collected over the decades. The Sergeant he'd roped in—Ulman—was a twenty year veteran with golden hash marks for meritorious service on his sleeve. Each of his men were past their ten. In spite of the fact that I outranked three of them and was even older than one, I still felt positively juvenile in their company.

We got back on the road after a quick meeting that I skipped in favor of grabbing us some more coffee from a street vendor. Thief was quiet as he drove. He stopped being completely silent only to sip his coffee, and even that was done in a more subdued manner than was his wont. I considered asking him about the plan, but was afraid if I knew exactly what we were up to that it might mean actually having to inform Trawler and request an intervention.

So I mimicked my partner and stayed silent while watching the dark streets slide on by.

Our tour started with a bakery on Finger Lane in Kaid's Cross. It was one of the front businesses owned by Tandem Holdings, and by virtue of that, we had every right to search it and question the employees.

I hadn't believed the scope when I'd first read the warrant, so I'd gone back a few times. It was clear, and the broadest document I'd seen in my career.

Hargold wasn't fooling around when he said he'd been calling in favors.

We strolled into the store as they were starting to roll out the last of the morning's pastries and loaves. Hargold and I flashed our sigils to get attention, and stepped up past the handful of customers waiting to grab something before work.

He asked for the manager and we waited as one of the clerks wandered away. The officers cleared the customers out.

Sergeant Ulman locked the door.

I'm not sure what I'd expected to happen after that. If I'd actually thought about it, I probably would have seen it coming. In my defense, I was exhausted.

"What're you doing? Why are you kicking my customers out?" asked a squat, red-faced dwarf as he walked out of the back.

"We have a warrant to search...and interrogate," said Thief as he waved the papers.

The dwarf blinked. "Huh?"

Hargold grinned at the man. It was a predatory look. I'd

seen it a few times, and it never worked out well for the person being smiled at. "I have a question," said the veteran detective. "Answer it and we leave right now."

"What?"

"I need to get in touch with your boss."

"He's not in on Fridays. Can I—"

"You misunderstand me," said Thief as he leaned across the counter. "I want to know how to get in touch with your boss at Tandem Holdings."

The dwarf's eyes blinked rapidly. "Never heard of it. My boss—"

"Toss it," said my partner.

So they did.

I've done a few prison cell searches for cases where someone inside was up to their neck in a murder. I know what a good, demoralizing search is meant to look like.

The uniforms went overboard.

Within seconds they'd spread out. Two in the front of the shop, two in the back. Everything started to hit the floor. The fresh bread. The register. The coffeemaker. Everything.

I started to open my mouth but Hargold grabbed me and pulled me over to the door. "Do. Not. Open. Your. Fucking. Mouth." He shoved me against the wall and walked back over to the counter.

The dwarf was going crazy. He was screaming at the officers. Screaming at Thief. He even tried screaming at me.

Five minutes later my partner sat down at one of the small tables lining the walls and started leafing through the paperwork the Sergeant had recovered from the back. I sat down across from him and took half the stack from him. He raised his eyebrows and I shrugged.

Front or not, the bakery employed civilians and served a neighborhood. So it wasn't that I was buying into my partner's methodology. I just wanted something to take my mind off the racket.

Shortly after six we unlocked the door and walked out. Sergeant Ulman argued—loudly—that we should move on to Tandem's Black Spit fronts. Thief told him that heading to Seaward to find some classier properties to shake down was the way to go, and he was in charge, so why didn't the Sarge just go fuck himself.

In the end, we weren't any wiser as to who was behind Tandem. But then Hargold wasn't finished with his favors.

Not by a long shot.

We sat in the Hallowstone drinking more coffee. The brew had been obtained from a completely different bakery, and I'd taken the opportunity to grab some chocolate bread. When bacon isn't possible, chocolate bread will do.

"What were you thinking?" I asked as I chewed a soft, warm mouthful of my breakfast combination.

He shrugged. "Shake the tree, see if any nuts fall out?"

I swallowed, then chased the remnants with a sip of the coffee. "We're not even sitting on them to see where they run to."

"Anonymous mailboxes? No offices? This isn't an organization run on face-to-face chatter, Dire."

"So he'll chime. We're not sitting on him. We won't know what's going on."

Hargold shook his head. "I'm sitting on that idiot dwarf's fucking head and he doesn't even know it. He's already been played."

"Wha—"

"Hargold, it's Mac," said a voice over the link, cutting me off. No contact protocol. I wrinkled my brow and checked the display. It indicated central.

"Who'd he call?" asked my partner.

"Female voice answered, transferred your guy right through. He reported in, sounded pretty shaken if you ask me. Male voice on the other end told him to make the joint disappear."

"Call the Fire Brigade. Tell them they've got an arson pending in Kaid's Cross. Finger Lane, number 125."

"Already done. I've sent the address the clarion trace brought

106

up to your golem too."

"Thanks, Mac."

"Hey, Thief."

"Yeah?"

"I hope you get the bastards that killed your friend. Catch a drink sometime soon, right?"

My partner grinned. "Oh, I will. And I'm buying after I do."

The link cut out, and Hargold stopped talking. I triggered the unit's golem, overriding the voice navigation and plotting a route to the newest address forwarded from central. Hargold glanced at the directions and eased the carriage out into traffic. Our blue and white escorts slid in behind without needing to be told.

I looked out the window and watched my city roll by as day broke.

Heartcore is all upscale, of course. There's not a run-down section in the entire ward, which is more than you can say for just about anywhere in the city proper outside of The Narrows. All the New Dagonian governmental buildings—the national ones, at least—are in Heartcore. Embassies from hundreds of the Thousand Kingdoms have a presence as well.

It's the second largest ward in the entire metropolis, and that's saying something. In fact, the ward is so large that it has three NDPD watchtowers. There are thousands of officers assigned just to Heartcore patrols. There is no safer place in the nation.

Heartcore's watchtowers are even run by a semi-autonomous Deputy-Chief. They don't interact with the rest of us all that often. Their watchtower detectives handle specialty work when they can get away with it as well. The number of cases I've worked in the ward during my career can be counted on barely two hands, and they've all been high profile.

So it's the perfect place to run your money laundering business, really. Nobody is looking for that kind of crime. Outside of the detectives in the FCD and OCU, cops aren't really interested in laundering operations. Since OCU is in Hammersmith, and Timberhold is home to the Fraud Squad and the other desk jockeys with sigils, that leaves nobody on the ground in Hammersmith to hassle folks like Tandem Holdings, even if they knew where it was actually located.

I'd been developing a sense of dread as we got closer to our destination. Not a lot of businesses outside of the service industry are run in Heartcore. If it doesn't have to do with governing or supporting the business of governing, there simply isn't any room.

Which is why I wasn't surprised at all when we rolled up outside of somewhere very bad indeed.

"We are not going in there," I said. "I'll call Trawler and have you locked up for your own good rather than risk you starting an invasion."

"Griff, that's where the call was picked up." Hargold was visibly agitated as he stared at the facade of the embassy belonging to the Republic of Sallee. "That's where the bastards who have all the answers are."

"If they're in there, we can't go get them. And if they aren't New Dagonian, all we can do is revoke visas and send them home even if they come outside." I poked him in the shoulder. "That's if we can get someone at central to sign off on it. And they'll probably have to find an ally in the Foreign Office to cover their own butts."

"They know why Murder is dead. If they didn't do it themselves."

"We don't know that."

"I fucking feel it," he said. His voice was strained.

"Look, let's—"

"He was in Sallee when he chimed, Griff." Thief put his hands together. "I know I'm asking a lot, but this is my last fucking day on the Job. My last chance to get the bastards who did this to my oldest friend." He choked up, then shook his head as he cleared his throat. "I need my partner."

"Ah bugger me, Hargold." I shook my head. "Fucking fine, you daft bastard. But I swear to you, if I lose my thrice-damned sigil over your shit I will haunt you for the rest of your days."

"Deal." He extended his meaty paw and I took it. He shook my hand not with the crushing grip he used to good effect all too regularly, but with the firm, even pressure of the man I'd come to realize I would gladly hand over my life for.

"So, you loon, do you have anything like a plan?"

For a man bent on serving justice—or, if it came to it, vengeance—Thief remained as calculating as ever. We spread our uniforms out over a few blocks surrounding the embassy. Close enough to call if we needed them, but not so close that they looked out of place.

Hargold had vanished to go chime a handful of contacts, and when he'd come back twenty minutes later we played a waiting game. Yet as we idled, the seeming inexhaustible supply of favors continued to work its magic.

One of the markers he'd called in paid off within a quarter of an hour. A detailed listing of the personnel at the embassy came via a courier service, direct to our unit.

I assumed the packet came directly from someone at the Foreign Office, which was unusual given that NDPD detectives have very little contact with those in the halls of power. When I pressed him for the details of how he'd pulled it off, he just stonewalled me and scoured the papers.

"Small staff," he said, pointing to the thin file. "See here. Most of them are even New Dagonian." He shook his head. "I'm tempted to eliminate them."

"I don't know if we need to eliminate them outright, but I do like someone from Sallee for this," I said. "Their central government is weak. The entire nation is mainly run by local powers, and most of those have a reputation for corruption. There are strong criminal families operating as good as openly across the country."

"When did you get a briefing?"

"University." I smiled. "Some of us actually have an education, remember?"

"Some of us grew up trying to stay alive." He winced almost immediately after spitting the words out. "Shit, Griff, I'm sorry."

"It's ok, brother." Me being orphaned at eight had meant a childhood of trying to survive without family. I'd been cared for by the Kaledonian state, of course. But there's only so much a government can do for a boy whose kin—whose *entire village*—were erased from the land by the waking cycle of an elder dragon. "I know you were just needling me. Now, about the Salleeans?"

He tapped the stack. "We have six of them."

"Illuminations?"

"Yes." He handed the images over. I leafed through them. They consisted mostly of surveillance footage shot in various governmental buildings, but also in restaurants and other public places.

"Hold on, these are from Foreign Office?"

"I never said that."

"Hargold, this isn't official, above-the-board stuff. Half of these are surreptitiously shot. This shit is absolutely not from the Foreign Office."

"Perceptive, but I wasn't always a cop, was I?"

I looked at the man I thought I knew and wrinkled my nose at him. "Who in the bloody Kingdoms are you, man?"

He shrugged, and declined to answer.

"None of them look much like our sketch. Maybe this guy," I said, tapping one of the pictures. "But he looks very young."

"No, you're right, their files don't look right either. Damn." He started to look through the stack of dossiers on the New Dagonians.

I pointed at the rest of the illuminations. "If you're looking for a connection there, go ahead and give me those."

He handed them over and went back to reading. I began to flip through the pictures.

Thief flicked a page with his finger, making it pop. "Hello! This—"

"—one." I finished, holding up an illumination of a middle-aged man with a scar down his cheek.

He nodded. "Lannik Mann. Salleean born; but to New Dagonian parents. Raised in Sallee, and educated in New Dagonia. Never renounced his citizenship here." Thief tapped the man's records with two thick fingers. "This fucker is around the right age to have run with Murder. He's only a couple years younger than I am."

"He's got the right background to be tied into a Salleean syndicate." I smiled and tilted my head. "Smart, really. Looking for the perfect way to diversify and get your syndicate's hands on foreign property? Recruit foreign operatives."

"One problem still," he said.

"No proof."

"Not a shred."

"We could put him in front of the old lady," I said.

"He'd walk. She only caught a second of him, and if he's as connected as we think, he has money enough to wiggle free."

I nodded. I'd known the idea was no good when I'd suggested it. "We sweat him?"

"A deep cover criminal-slash-spy operating on foreign turf? Not too likely to crack if you ask me."

"Do you have a better plan?"

He looked the file over, flipping between the pages which detailed Mann's history. "Huh. Maybe." He pointed to a line in the file. "What's that look like to you?"

I shrugged. "An anomaly."

"And when I show you this?" He held up staff member's another file and tapped midway down the page.

"Opportunity," I said, and gave him a grin.

CHAPTER 10

"**H**ey, I was thinking; if this works I might not even lose my sigil and need to sleep on your couch," I said into my link. I was still in the Hallowstone a half a block from the embassy, tucked into an alley. I'd managed to find some more coffee and a veggie wrap while we were setting up our operation, so I was in a pretty good mood.

"You whine a lot for a grown man." Hargold was sitting a few blocks away, at the counter of a local restaurant. He was watching Mann and a woman in her mid-30's we'd pegged as Kimara Deurn, one of the embassy's clarion operators. Deurn was also a New Dagonian.

The pair were having lunch and flirting. Kimara's file indicated that she was married—not to Lannik, of course—and that her husband was routinely away on business. It also gave a list—a long one—of men she was enjoying regular affairs with. Most of them were also suspected foreign intelligence operatives.

Whether they were working her, she was working them, or she just liked a lot of sex was unclear. But she did have a standing lunch date with Mann on Fridays. That was our opening.

What I found most interesting was that Lannik was not on the extensive list of foreign operatives who regularly pumped her. For information or otherwise. As far as her file was concerned he was just one of a few New Dagonians she was intimate with on a regular basis. Considering what we knew of his activities and his background, it looked a lot like someone had screwed that assessment up.

My new working theory—which I'd generated as I sipped my coffee and tried to control the rising jitters—was that the files came from the Bureau of Intelligence. Also, that the BI analyst who had prepared the file on the embassy had grossly misidentified our man as being unremarkable.

"She's moving." Hargold's warning wasn't for me; it was for Falcon. He and Rabino were out the side exit of the restaurant, ready to squeeze Deurn hard the second she was away from Mann's side.

"I see her," said Bird. A moment later he came across the void again. "Rabino has her. Running interference."

"Mann's just gotten up too," said Hargold, "watch it."

I bit my cheek as my pulse spiked. We needed time for Rabino to work the woman over. He'd been chosen because he's the most likable of us all, and he's a genius with devices.

Originally Falcon had wanted me to handle her; pour on the charm. Thief had quashed the idea because seduction took time. He wanted to make her an offer, and Rabbit was the one of us she'd be least likely to refuse.

"He's taking a leak," said Falcon.

"Handle him," Thief said, voice tight.

"I'm not handling him while he's got his pants down."

I expected a bark from my partner. He opened up his link on a laugh instead. "Sorry, Bird. I know you've got him."

A minute of silence passed. I was too far away to know if anything was actually happening. The carriage wasn't even parked in line of sight to the restaurant. I drummed on the wheel of the unit to relax myself, and started to sing a little song as I waited for feedback.

"He's headed back," said Falcon less than a minute later.

"He reacted to her not being there," said Thief. "He's looking for her."

"We're live," said Rabbit. "Get in there and do what I told you, you'll be fine."

"I'll try," said a female voice—Kimara Deurn—over the scryer Rabino had fitted her with. She seemed calm, which was fairly amazing given what Rabino had likely told her would happen if she didn't play along.

"You'll do great."

"She's going in now," said Falcon. "We're backing off. You're on your own, you cranky old man."

"Thanks," said Thief.

"Sorry, where were we?" asked Kimara.

"What took you so long?" Mann sounded irritated.

"The dryer wasn't working right. It was blowing cold, so it took forever."

"So, the two embassy luncheons next week—"

"Oh, right, of course." She laughed. The woman was a natural talent. I found her convincing, and I knew she was transmitting. "I have entertainment booked, of course. Say, I tried to get in touch with that one musician. The soloist the ambassador liked so much last month. I know he's a New Dagonian, middle aged, dark hair."

"Who?"

"Oh, you know. The one with the song about the sorrowful seas." She giggled and hummed a few bars. "Ugh, remembering is murder sometimes."

"What?" Something clattered.

"Oh, Lannik. It's right in front of me. I could just shoot myself." She was amazing. Even more, Rabino was amazing. He'd had less than five minutes to talk her into the sting, prep her, and get her linked in.

"What the—," a loud noise came across the scryer. "I have to go."

"Sweetie, where are you—"

A muffled thud sounded. "Watch yourself," said Thief. "I'm standing right here."

Mann started out hot. "You watch—," he cut off and softened his tone as he got a look at who he'd run into. "Yeah, I will, sorry."

"He's out in the open," said Thief.

"I have his transmission," Rabbit said. "Linking him in now

for tracking, and cutting the girl's feed. Where'd you put it, Thief?"

"It's in his pocket."

"Won't have good audio. I'll cut that channel."

"I'm taking Deurn in," said Falcon.

"No, just hand her off to patrol one," I said. "We need you back in the game."

He laughed. "Oh trust me, nobody fucks with Homicide Unit. I'm in the game."

"Going to miss your ass, Bird," said Thief. There was a moment of silence before he reported in again. "I'm moving."

Seconds ticked by. "He's headed towards you, Griff," said Rabino. "You're up."

I slipped out of the carry and peeked around the corner of the alley. I could barely make Mann out just past the hackney queue down a block. "I see him."

"I hope this works."

"Me too Rabbit." I let my wand slide free of the spring sheath up my sleeve. I held it tightly next to my leg as I broke cover and made double time towards the embassy.

The guards at the gate were typical New Dagonian security personnel. The companies that contract for the embassies have no actual authority to do anything but ensure that their assigned buildings are defended. It was a fair bet that what I was about to do wouldn't be immediately fatal.

But they were armed, and accidents do happen. My pulse started to race. Too much coffee. The spirit within me stirred, reacting to my stress. I pushed it down as I raised my weapon.

"Die Salleean scum!" I discharged my wand—far over the guards' heads—as I shouted. "Criminal bastards!" I aimed at a statue yards away from the steps to the embassy and watched the guards make a hasty retreat into the embassy. "Syndicate goons!" I sent another shot at the now vacant steps.

The doors to the building slammed and the automated gates in front of me swung slowly but inexorably shut. I continued ranting at the gates and firing on the building. Standard issue ice wands are terrible at penetrating cover. I wasn't endangering anyone.

"He's spotted you," said Thief. "He stopped."

My link flared to life as a new channel opened. "072707. Dispatch. Shots fired in your vicinity."

I ignored dispatch and waved my wand, firing it wildly. "Filthy degenerates!" I reloaded with a fresh crystal before blowing off more charge. "Tyrannical despots!"

"We have him trapped out in the open," said Rabbit "He's got to jump soon."

"Bloody good," I said. "Can I stop firing yet?"

"He's headed back towards me," said Thief. "You're good to go."

"In fact," said Falcon, "I'd start going now."

"What?" I asked.

"Dispatch didn't buy that we've handled the situation. They won't call off the Heartcore units." I heard the sirens closing in as he said it. "You should start running, Dire. Now."

I didn't wait to be told twice.

CHAPTER 11

The Heartcore patrols responding to my attack on the Sal-leean embassy were quick to get to the scene. I wasn't surprised given the typical density of units in the ward; but their punctuality didn't work in my favor.

Not in the least.

The first unit to respond came at me from the direction Mann had disappeared. The blue and white wove towards me through traffic, which had come to a screeching halt when I'd started my assault. In the aftermath of the incident, people were ducked down in their vehicles. Progress for the officers was slow, but even so, the stoppage was worth scant extra seconds.

Which would have been fine—since my preferred route was back towards the Hallowstone—but I hadn't even finished turning before a uniform on foot emerged from the alley.

Blocked both up and down the avenue, I took the only other real route available.

I launched myself over the hood of the carry parked in the embassy's loading zone and darted through the open spaces the drivers had afforded me when they'd started cowering.

"Halt! NDPD!"

I ignored the officer and slid between two parked carries as I reached the other side of the avenue. My knees naturally bent and I hunched over anticipating his fire. Impossibly hard chunks of ice, compressed by the magic of his service wand struck the wall behind me as he unleashed.

The slivers of ice blew out the windows of the carries I was running behind. I felt the shock of pain as I took some glass to my face. Fortunately I'd closed my eyes at the right moment to avoid blindness; but I could taste blood from my cut lip, and the metallic smell of fresh injuries flooded my nose.

An alleyway yawned in front of me. I rolled from cover into it. Shards of ice impacted around me, striking a rubbish bin as I ducked behind it.

"Unarmed!" I called out. Not that I expected the officer to slow down, but it was worth a try. I didn't stick around to see if he would moderate his aggression.

I broke out of the crouch and ran.

My sprint was flat-out for about ten seconds. The alleyway flew by. Filth mixed with blood hovered in my nose; a wild pulse hammered in my throat. I could see a fire escape ahead, on my right. Far beyond it, another street loomed.

I was halfway down the passageway when my beast stirred in its cage. The spirit woke with a fury in it. I had to force myself to hold steady in the face of its rage. Moments later it screeched a warning.

Ice flew past my head as I dropped to the ground and slid through the refuse, skinning my hands and tearing my trousers. "Stop!" shouted the officer.

I declined. I spotted a door with peeling red paint to my left. Leaping to my feet, I rushed it. I checked the handle.

Not locked. I ripped it open and heard the impact of blasts on the portal as I dove in.

The griffon tore at me as I navigated the building, demanding I give it control. It clawed to get out as I mounted a staircase a few yards in.

With a shove, I beat the creature back down and felt it recede. I'd never forced it back down so hard before; but I wasn't chasing enemies, and all my totem knew was the hunt.

I began to climb hard, taking the treads two at a time. I could feel the blood running down my face as my pulse raced, fueling my flight.

Fight. Survive. Fly.

I felt it still, deep inside. But as I climbed, I pushed the longings of the spirit aside. No matter how much the little wanker in pursuit was pissing me off, he didn't deserve what the beast would do to him.

The stairs ended on the fourth floor with no roof access. Not that I really wanted a rooftop chase, but it would have meant being able to see. I burst through the door, startling the office workers who dotted the cubicles across the floor.

"Where the fuck are you?" asked Thief over the link.

"Across." I leapt over the short partition in front of me and flipped the desk of a gnome over, startling the poor woman. "Sorry," I said as I hauled the furniture up against the doorway.

"Across?" asked my partner.

"From the embassy." I grabbed another desk and upended it. A slight, middle-aged human backed away as I removed his workspace. "Very sorry," I said as I gave him a smile and blocked off the door.

"What building?"

"Alley," I said as I abandoned my makeshift barricade and started to run towards the door on the opposite side of the room. "Red door."

"Helpful, Dire."

"Bugger off." I attempted to hop a mail cart and wound up knocking it over. Piles of envelopes and stacks of packages scattered across the floor. "Sorry!" I called out as I fled.

A crash behind me was followed by renewed orders from the uniform. I kept running towards the exit before me, without ducking. He couldn't fire without risking civilians at this point.

I made my way into the stairwell to the sound of his shouts, and slammed the door behind me. I looked down the steps, then up them, towards the roof.

Maybe it was the beast guiding me, but I suddenly found myself choosing the high ground.

☆ ☆ ☆ ☆ ☆

"On the roof," I said into my link as I burst out into the sunshine again. Afternoon heat struck me as I blinked and oriented myself.

"Get cover," said Thief. "Rabino says ATU is incoming."

"Arse." I looked up at the sky to see if I could spot any of the automatons. "How long?"

"Three minutes." There was a pause before he amended himself. "Maybe less."

"How many on foot?" I asked as I scanned the rooftop. A few chairs were scattered around. Cigarettes lay strewn across the area, butts rolled in dozens of different styles.

"A beat cop and three patrol units inside—or closing on—your building," said Thief after a few seconds.

I was about to ask him for details when the door slammed open, revealing my original pursuer. He blinked in the sun and raised his wand.

My hand shot out and slapped the uniform's wrist wide as he discharged the weapon. Ice flew into empty space across the rooftops.

Spinning in, I slammed my left elbow into his solar plexus. Air burst forth from him in a loud cough and he dropped forward, over my back.

I stripped the wand with my right hand and grabbed his collar with my left. Shifting my weight and dropping to a knee I hauled him up and over my back.

The beat cop slammed into the rooftop in front of me. He struggled to get his breath back even as he tried to turn and fight. I moved with him, slipped in behind, and locked my right arm around his neck.

"Don't fight, I'm not going to hurt you, mate," I said as he started to struggle against the neck hold. "Relax." He flailed a bit then lost consciousness.

I laid him out on the rooftop and checked his breathing. It was a bit ragged from the blow to the gut, but still strong.

"Time?" I asked.

"Less than two. Lead patrol is on the third. Beat should be on you."

"He's neutralized."

"Then stop thinking and move your ass."

"Aye." I ran to the near edge of the building. Looking out in the direction of the diner—and my squad—all I could see was the crowded street below. No fire escape to be seen.

The escape on the embassy side would be too dangerous, so I headed to the opposite corner and checked to see if there was any egress available.

No bones.

"Griff! You have fucking seconds to get inside."

I could hear the approaching screams of the ATU automatons. I scanned the sky but still couldn't see any sign of the drones. If I was lucky they'd just be loaded out for typical acquisition and tracking. All air units are enchanted to seek out perpetrators and keep tabs on them.

They're very effective.

Still, being hunted by an incredibly efficient drone was a more pleasant experience than what would happen if they were armed. ATU standard attack loadouts were usually lethal, and even the less-than-lethal weaponry they fitted the automatons with was potentially deadly. I'd seen a rooftop standoff go badly when an LTL round knocked a man off the edge to his death.

I turned and ran full tilt at the far side of the building, headed towards the fire escape on the far side of the alley I'd entered from. The high-pitched whine announcing the imminent arrival of ATU support was getting louder by the second. I searched for the top of the fire escape on the building ahead of me, but couldn't see it.

"Stop!" Not wasting any time waiting on a response, the newly-arrived patrol unit, which had just spotted me, opened fire.

Ice flew, striking the edge of the roof behind me, the rooftop at my feet, and a bench I passed at a dead run.

I aimed for where I thought the fire escape might be. Fifteen yards to go. Blasts flew into the space beyond me as I pumped my arms, duster flying out behind me. A few of the slivers struck the short wall in front of me. I was a long way off from the officers, but the angle was getting better for them as I closed on my chosen spot. The projectiles were zeroing in.

Three things happened so close together they seemed to blur into one.

My partner, voice strained, broke in over the void. "You're out of time, Griff."

The loud whine of the first ATU unit silenced as it broke hard from approach speed and started to hunt.

And a strangely muted pain spread across my back as I was struck by a blast in the shoulder blade.

All of it seemed very odd indeed as my consciousness began to fade just as I cleared the roof's low wall and pushed off into thin air.

CHAPTER 12

When I think back, I guess it was the falling which kept me from passing out. The weird drop in my gut kept me from not quite going black as I arced across the gap.

I'd aimed mostly well without being able to see the structure as I'd approached. My trajectory carried me towards the corner of the escape on the fourth floor of the building. Unfortunately I was angled to the outside, and not the landing.

The impact as I struck the bars was devastating.

I felt my wrist shatter as my left arm instinctively shot out to catch hold of the metal. I screamed then. I think. My right arm flailed almost uselessly, half crippled from the shot I'd taken.

"Griff," said someone. The voice seemed anxious. And far away.

I decided I was too busy falling to care.

The next level went better. If 'better' is only wrenching your knee and spraining an ankle as you slam into the edge blind.

I'm not sure how I managed it, but I hooked the other leg into the railing and halted my progress. I felt it strain but nothing further popped or broke.

I hung—upside down—three floors off the alleyway with a broken wrist, a twisted knee, and a sprained ankle.

Not to mention the hole in my back.

Oh, and my face was pouring blood again as it rushed to the open wounds.

So, what else was I going to do? I started laughing.

124

That's when the griffon got out.

Fight?
Fight!
Pain!
Danger.
Fly!
Fly?
Clipped.
Run!

For the first time, in near three decades of living with it, I realized that I still had access to all of my senses as the totem moved me.

I could see the inverted world, and my duster dangling from me. The sound of the blood hammering in my head, and the whine of the circling automaton were clear. I could smell my own sweaty fear, and the blood in my mouth; blood which tasted like a blade between my teeth.

Worst of all, I could feel.

The agony as the beast forced my limbs to perform was maddening. The sensation of the bones in my wrist grinding together as my body scrabbled for purchase against my will was sickening. My back pulsed with slick torment and stabbed bright lances of hurt through me as I found myself hauled upright by foreign impulses.

I wanted to scream; but I was a prisoner, and the spirit refused to bow to the hurt.

Fucking spirit.

It managed to use my ravaged appendages to haul the rest of

me up and over the railing. As my body rolled over the barrier, I expected to collapse on the landing and rest.

Apparently totems are callous about their bonded needing to pause, because no respite came.

The thrice-damned thing lashed out with my injured leg, using the hale one to balance, and smashed through the glass of the window in one go. I expected to fall down and bleed to death, but it extricated my limb from the pane deftly, and kicked a large remnant free.

Within a few seconds, it slapped the last two vicious looking pieces of glass free, sending agonizing jolts through my shoulder, and hopped through the gaping portal.

It discovered a stairwell just inside and started down it. The run it broke into as it tore down the steps two at a time made me wish I couldn't feel anything. The ankle and knee were holding, but it seemed as if one or both might buckle at any moment. I was certain that it would need to stop soon.

But the beast was undaunted.

The sub-basement of the building is where it stopped, finally. I wanted to drop and curl into a ball; the five flights had taken their toll on me. But that's not why it paused. It was listening.

The sensation was similar to when I let it roam outside of me, but subtly different. More powerful, perhaps. I could hear the drops of moisture falling from pipes nearby, and the hum of air in the vents. Hot or cold, I wasn't sure, but the swishing of the currents sounded like flight to my hybridized hearing.

Mundane things weren't what my totem was listening for though. Its keen hearing outmatched my ability to process, but the feeling of danger and the confusion it felt at being hunted were clear.

Griffons aren't prey. The spirit was doing what it could to flee, but its first instinct was to fight, and it couldn't. The growing frustration—and borderline hysteria—had the totem in a quandary.

Police officers aren't usually prey either, so I could empathize.

As the seconds grew longer, I started to wonder just how paralyzed by the situation the spirit was. I'd never been aware when it was in control before, but all reports of its—or my— behavior during those times pointed at direct action.

Fighting. Fleeing. Things the totem was good at.

So far it had fled, but cornered itself. Now, stuck in a hole— injured to boot—it just sat, and listened. Time was running out.

"Give me my body back," I thought at it.

Danger! The response was like a chill running up my spine. More a feeling—or even an emotion—than language.

"We'll be captured if we don't flee." I concentrated my thoughts on a big cage. Something large enough for a griffon to be contained in.

Trapped.

My heart sunk as the spirit's dismay rolled through me. I fought against the despair.

"Give me control."

Defend. Protect. Fierce waves of pride and loyalty assaulted me. It was almost enough to make me shed a tear.

Almost.

"Get. Back. Inside." I pushed with every bit of willpower I had, forcing the totem beast back towards its refuge. It fought mightily, but I kept my focus tight. Like my father had taught me when I was just a littlin on his knee.

With one last thrust, I backed the spirit down and slammed shut the door to its domain. I panted and felt a smile crack my face as I realized I'd been the one to decide that I was back in control for the first time in my life. That sensation was short-lived though.

A few seconds of quiet elation was all I managed before the crush of the pain slammed into me, and I buckled.

CHAPTER 13

"**D**ire, can you hear me?"

I fluttered my eyes open in the dark of the sub-basement and groaned. I turned my head and felt a sticky puddle against my beard.

"Damn, Griff, where are you?" Thief's voice was less strained than it had been, but he sounded worried enough still.

I forced my right hand to trigger the link. Pain in my shoulder seemed less sharp. I wanted to consider that fact a good thing, only I was concerned about how much blood I was lying in. "Here," I said in a voice that didn't seem to want to come out.

"They've lost you in the building you jumped to, but they're unloading the dogs now."

"Blind."

"You're blind?"

I laughed. It hurt, but I felt better for it. "They are. I'm bleeding pretty bad. They should have a clear trail without dogs."

There was silence for a few seconds before Hargold came back across the void. "Turn yourself in," he said in a subdued voice.

"What?"

"Don't get yourself killed."

"You come up with this mad plan to flush Mann out and—" I broke off and lay there thinking.

"Griff?"

"Where are you?"

"Falcon and I are shadowing Mann. We left Rabino behind to collect you, but he can't get ahead of the search. The second patrol unit is out there too, but they absolutely can't engage in Heartcore." He was quiet for a minute and I could hear his tight breathing over the link. "Turn yourself in, Griffon. Better alive and looking for a job than dead and not needing one. You can sleep on my couch forever for all I care."

I stared at the dimly lit ceiling for a few moments. I was dizzy. I was tired. There was still a lot of pain going on.

There was a chance that I was in real danger.

But there was also the chance that I'd pull through on my own. Maybe better than just a chance.

"Rabbit needs to find me a way out of the sub-basement. Sewer, chute, or anything else. They'll be coming for me soon and I need to be gone."

"What the—"

"Tell him, Hargold. Find me a way out."

"You die and I'll kill you," he said. Then he cut the link on me.

I took a few deep breaths and kept the rhythm they afforded me as I steadied myself. In through the nose, then out through the mouth.

Next I sought something that didn't exist. A single point of focus—not a place in the real world—appeared to me as I opened myself to it. A conduit through which I could absorb the energy I'd need.

It was hidden. Halfway between myself and nowhere. I sensed it, and let my focus drift around that point I couldn't see.

Then I let the griffon loose.

It leapt from me, screeching its agitation. I rebuked it gently and willed it to gather energy for a spell. As it rushed away to find a source I heard a noise from the stairwell.

It was just a few moments later when I realized the sound was dogs barking.

CHAPTER 14

I felt my heart pound harder as the spirit sped into the distance. The dogs got louder as the seconds rushed away from me.

I wondered if they'd rip me to pieces before I got a chance to surrender. It usually didn't happen—CPU officers were well-disciplined, and so were most of their animals—but I was still bleeding profusely.

"Dire," said Rabino over the link.

I felt myself tense up, with predictably painful results. "Rabbit. Please give me good news." I tried not to sound desperate. I'm fairly sure I failed.

"In the corner of the sub-basement is a chute which leads up into the main body of the building."

"Which corner? Where's it come out?"

"There are openings on every floor, including the fourth, which is currently empty. Head away from the stairwell to the wall. It'll be on your right."

"Any way you can get up there?"

He paused for a moment. "Within five. Can you climb?"

"I'm so buggered I can barely walk, but I'm working on it."

"See you soon." The link died again.

The next thirty seconds were lonely. The dogs were alerting regularly, and I was getting sleepy. I wondered if playing dead worked as well with police dogs as it did with bears. I wondered if there were any bears at the pub. Maybe they'd buy me a drink. What would the bears drink? Mead. Of course. So obvious.

As the spirit returned power flowed into me through the narrowing conduit, jolting me back into full consciousness.

"Now, you bastard." I hauled myself up into a sitting position. "You're going to help me do this."

We'd been bonded since I was a child; the griffon had subtly aided me without being guided for decades. I knew that together we would be stronger. The spirit had never been able to manipulate a great deal of power on its own; but I'm what they call a prodigy in New Dagonia, and that makes me a raw talent capable of using ley energy directly.

Now I took the power it had found for me and beckoned to the spirit. I reached out for the beast, mustering every bit of my will as I coaxed it to assist me. I'd decided to test our bond by offering the totem more energy than it could draw itself. All I asked it to do was something it had done hundreds of times before.

Namely to speed my recovery from injury.

Instead of letting the griffon handle knitting a bone a couple weeks early, or making a cut fade after a day or two, I was giving it enough power to restore my health immediately.

I hoped.

As we made the connection I felt its understanding. The results were at once less, and more spectacular than I had imagined.

Ley energy surged through me as I forced the conduit wide open. Maybe the beast can't manipulate much power, but it has the ability to find and gather a great deal. The seemingly endless torrent of raw magical energy poured through me, threatening to sweep me away.

I'm a piss-poor wizard when compared to the greats of bygone eras. The legendary Auromyth would have no doubt laughed to see me struggle with the spell I'd prepared.

But Auromyth and his kind were a thousand years gone. Natural talents like myself were nearly extinct; our lines nearly eradicated by the purges of the intervening centuries. Plus, my father was dead, cutting off that route to knowledge.

Finally, orphans who knew enough to hide their talents were never plucked out of their dreary lives to be educated in lofty private institutions. I'd thus avoided the preparation for a presumably thrice-damned boring career developing the latest new devices for one of the mighty conglomerates.

But I did what I could, and shaped the energy to my will. The spirit lent its own innate skill to my efforts, and together we crafted something new. I let the current flow between us; felt the arcing power rush from myself to the totem, and back again.

Truth be told, I was completely winging it.

After a brief flurry of power, the conduit did in fact run out of raw energy, and the power faded as it sunk into me. I felt warmth. Comfort. And then the magic was gone.

All at once I felt eight again. Like I was running through the heather in the meadows, chasing my mates and playing at soldiers. I imagined laughing with them and talking about the midsummer bonfires when we'd sneak some drinks and maybe catch a peek at the big fire on the hill, where all the older lads and lasses went for the night.

Then a dog barked just up the stairs.

I thrust myself to my feet and ran.

CHAPTER 15

I was halfway across the sub-basement before I realized that running was a good sign. I'd made the chute by the time I connected my stride with the fact that I didn't have a scratch on me.

A quick feel at my face revealed that blood was still congealing on my face from vanished cuts, but my lips were whole again, and there was no fresh flow from any of the other wounds. My wrist moved freely and my leg was hale.

Elated from my success, and not wanting to wait and greet the handlers and their loyal partners, I crammed myself into the narrow metal tube and started to climb. It wasn't fast by any stretch, but I did manage to work my way up a couple feet at a time as I pressed my back into one side and my legs into the other.

I could hear the echoes of the Canine Presence Unit teams below me, but there was obvious confusion at the scene below. I kept climbing.

While I'd been healed by the spell it was only by the first floor that I realized I was fatigued. Whether from the lack of sleep or as some consequence of the magic, I started to shake from exhaustion before I'd cleared the second. At the third floor I considered just crawling out of the chute and taking my chances.

I'd nearly managed all six floors and could see the opening above my head, when my arm gave out as I pressed upward.

I started to slide away.

I caught myself before I went into free fall. But I was stuck, quivering, muscles screaming, just a few feet below the egress. I heard the dogs alerting below me and saw lights start to shine at the base of the chute. For a moment I imagined plummeting into the gathering below, scattering everyone like the pigeons in the square outside the orphanage had when I'd run through them early in the mornings.

"Grab my arm," said Rabino from just above me.

"Took you long enough," I said. I closed my eyes hard, then opened them, released the pressure of my right arm and flung it up towards him.

I slipped, of course.

And my squadmate caught me.

There was a minute of grunting and straining, and more foul language than usual. But together we managed to get me out of the chute without him joining me, and the pigeons below remained mercifully unscattered.

I lay panting on the floor of a hallway which was obviously in need of renovation. Rabino caught his breath quickly and started to unload a bag. "Put these on," he said.

A set of coveralls hit me and I rolled to start stripping my clothing off. I pulled my belongings out of my pockets and piled them up for transfer to the new clothes. "Do they have my face?"

"This saved you," he said as he plucked my fedora off and stuffed it in the bag.

"Lucky hat. I'll keep it forever."

"I would." He caught my duster, followed by torn trousers and shoes. "Underwear too in case of the dogs." He turned away and handed footwear over his shoulder. "Boots may be too small, sorry."

I took the pair and dropped them next to my feet. I winced at the inch of toe I wasn't going to be allowed to use. I stripped my shirt and underpants and chucked it beside him.

"We're going out the front door," Rabbit said as he started to splash water from a wall fountain over the contents of the bag. "This might dull a bit of the smell. Your clothes may be trashed, but you look better than I'd hoped. I was going to try and fake you as a casualty."

"Yeah. Long story."

"I bet."

It's not a secret that I'm gifted, but we don't talk about it much. Most people get uncomfortable when you do more than simple, child's play stuff like spark a light or make a small object float. The fourth—and hopefully final—Great Mage War was two hundred years ago, but those conflicts had made an impression.

Besides, what happened with the totem starting on the fire escape was a breakthrough, and I didn't know what to think yet.

So I stayed quiet, and he didn't ask again.

As I struggled into the boots I ribbed him. "I'm glad we didn't go with your casualty plan. It sucks."

"Would we have had much choice?"

"Not really. Don't look in the basement. It's not pretty."

When I was dressed in the DMU coveralls and had deposited my pile of sundries about my person I scrubbed my face and hands off in the fountain. Rabbit helped me spot blood I'd missed. Apparently I'd had a pretty nasty cut on my ear as well.

After I was presentable I put the DMU cap on and tucked my hair up to make it look shorter. We walked the length of the building to the far window. My feet hurt within ten yards and by the time we got to the exit I was gritting my teeth. We opened it—the polite way, not using my boots—and stepped onto the fire escape.

"Act like you're checking for blood."

"That's not hard. Look, here's splatter from when I missed the railing."

"I don't think you missed it with spray like that." He pointed and gave me a look that I took as acknowledgment of how disturbing it was that I wasn't bleeding any more.

"Yeah, ok, so now I'm pretending to follow the path of the fall."

"Good, because there's ATU making another pass." An automaton—one of the armed kind—buzzed past the alley. I looked back down from it and checked for more signs of my fall as I walked down the escape.

"Why aren't we going down into the alley?"

"We are."

"I thought you said the front door."

"Well, that's where I'm parked. It was convenient." He tilted his head and raised an eyebrow. "Did you expect me to jump across just to bust you out?"

I shook my head. "Turns out getting in that way is not a good plan."

We kept pointing and nodding at various blood evidence as we made our way down the structure. Another ATU drone passed us before we hit the alley, but it moved on. The NDPD wasn't interested in subjects not fitting the description of a badly bloodied, tall, dark-haired man; a man not wearing police coveralls, but a long, black coat, charcoal suit, and a fedora.

Still, after we rounded the corner of the alley and headed down the street I slouched the rest of the way to Rabino's unit.

Just in case.

CHAPTER 16

First order of business once we were clear of the scene was getting me all the way cleaned up and into some actual clothes. Rabbit dropped two hundred liri on the desk of one of the executive health clubs that dot Heartcore just for the privilege of getting me a private shower. I was sure the club's owners wouldn't see a dime, but the cheerful young man who accepted Rabino's offer provided immediate access to a VIP locker room.

I stripped and bagged the disguise, then tossed it out the door. While my fellow second class took off to dispose of all the evidence—after I'd warned him that if either my hat or my coat came up missing in the end he'd suffer—and get me something to wear, I handled making myself presentable.

Showering the blood off of myself was harder than I'd expected. The stream was powerful and adjustable, as well as mercifully hot. But each time I thought I was finished another clump of dried fluid dislodged and spiraled towards the drain. I had blood clinging to places I hadn't even realized I'd injured.

It took nearly half an hour before I turned the water off and headed over to the mirror to survey myself. I stood naked and took stock. It was disturbing me to see just how perfect the healing was. My wrist showed no signs at all of ever having been snapped. I craned my neck to see the shoulder blade, sure that there would be a scar from the hole the shard of elemental ice had made. But it was pristine, and I couldn't feel a hitch or stiffness in the area.

I was just slipping my chrono on when Rabbit picked the

lock and slipped in. I flexed the wrist and marveled at the free-
dom of movement. 2:15PM hovered above my left palm.

"I didn't have a lot of time, so I did what I could. Found this
at a little boutique just across in Timberhold." He handed me a
shopping bag with a tartan pattern. "There's shoes in there that
should fit this time. I went maybe a touch large to be safe, but
there's two pair of socks if you have a problem."

I opened up the bag and started to pull things out. "We
need to be somewhere, I assume?"

"Yeah. Falcon checked in just before I got to the unit on my
way out. They're sitting on Mann—with all the uniforms—but
he hasn't reached out to anyone yet. So, the clock is ticking."

I looked through the clothes from the top half of the bag.
"They not sell underwear?"

"Don't worry, check the bundle at the bottom."

I rustled through the bag and pulled out a beautiful piece of
wool. "Not funny, Rabbit."

"Kaledonians don't wear anything beneath a kilt, do they?"

If my partner hadn't needed me I might have demanded different clothing. But Thief's friend was still dead, and our only
lead had apparently stopped panicking, and started to think.
Bad things happen when people have time to think.

"Aye, we don't," I said, dropping my towel. Rabino jerked
back as he got an eyeful, looked away, then looked back just a
second before shaking his head and closing his eyes.

"Damnit, Dire."

"Serves you right, bastard." I tugged the kilt up and started to fasten it. "Now, those had better be proper, knee-high
socks...."

Falcon waved as we got out of the carry and walked towards
a lorry tucked into another dingy alley—this time in Timberhold—which was serving as our operational command post.

He took a look at me and grinned. "Don't you look lov—"

"Shut it," I said, cutting him off. Thief glanced at me and grunted, but I noted the assessment as it happened; and caught the relaxation as he realized I wasn't going to drop dead.

"He does look mighty fine, laddie," said Rabino in his best—meaning, quite awful—Kaledonian burr.

"Who does his shopping?" asked Bird.

"Picked it out meself," said Prey with a bow. His accent didn't improve with practice.

"Very funny," said Thief. "Dire looks like a fucking piper in one of those stupid parades they always make us work overtime for."

Rabino dropped the burr. "Our wallets should thank him." The slender detective frowned a moment later. "Though my wallet is out a lot of liri. Don't suppose I can expense disguising a fugitive?"

"Good luck with that," I said. "I know that the lack of underwear alone means you won't see a penny from me." Falcon tilted his head at Rabino, but the junior detective just widened his eyes and shuddered. "What's the situation?" I asked my partner.

Hargold rubbed his hair back, and fluffed up the mane as best he could. "Mann ducked into the SRO down the way—Royal Arms, they call it—and got a key for 406. Desk clerk has the number to my man monitoring in dispatch, and the promise of a second hundred liri note if he lets us know if Mann moves."

I let the reference to the favor he'd called in alone and asked the obvious follow-up. "He have an in-room clarion?"

"No. Front desk can route to a few in the lobby alcove, but we have all three tapped." He pointed north then west. "Our backup is holding along the cross streets towards the gate sides, just in case Mann decides he's going to try and skip town."

"So they have eyes on?"

"Front door, yes."

"The back is that way," said Falcon, pointing down the alley.

"Green door on the right, end of the next alley. If he pokes his head out here then we'll know it.

"Long way off," I said straining to catch sight of the portal in question.

"The door is rigged for alarm." Falcon winked at me. "It sounds when anyone opens it."

I nodded. The door would be marked accordingly, so if Mann did leave he'd only take the back if he absolutely had to. "So, do we even have a plan?"

"We've flushed him out, and we can get at him." Thief tapped on the side of the lorry and shook his head. "DMU is at his apartment as we speak...."

"So, no actual plan outside of we can take him if we want to, and we're praying that some evidence leads back to Gallan."

"That's about right." My partner sighed and rubbed his face with both hands. "The problem is that we have no actual evidence. If we assume he's an operative of a Salleean criminal organization, it's safe to bet he's not going to crack just because we lean on him."

I shook my head. "By now he's possibly convinced himself that this was all a weird day, or that whoever is toying with him has no power, or no proof."

"Or both," said Rabbit.

"And unless he's sloppy, that DMU search will turn up empty." I swept my gaze across the others. "What would you do?"

"Get ready for a fight," said Thief.

Rabino shrugged. "Call for backup. Only he hasn't chimed anyone."

"Nope." Falcon yawned and took a sip of his drink. "He should have, but he hasn't."

There was silence as we worked things over. "How do we know for sure that he hasn't?" I asked after a minute.

"We sat on him the whole way. He didn't stop until he got to the Royal Arms. The clerk insists he just checked in and went to his room."

"What if he knew this was coming?" The question got me

curious looks. "I mean something bad, not this in specific. Like he had an escape plan."

"He's been operating in New Dagonia for years. Successfully, at that." Falcon said. "He probably does have a plan. But sitting in some SRO seems like a bad move."

"What if the SRO is a sign? What if that's the call for help?"

"Shit, Griff," said Thief. "If it is, he may be getting ready for a fight."

"Or to run," said Rabbit.

"What'd you tell the uniforms to look for?" I asked.

Hargold shrugged and frowned. "Just to watch for Mann, and anything else suspicious."

"What's not suspicious at the Royal Arms?"

He rubbed his beard for a moment before answering. "Tenants coming and going."

I nodded. "And how do we know who is a tenant, and who happens to be Mann's backup?"

"Fuck," said Falcon.

"Huh," Thief said as his face clouded over. "We don't.

CHAPTER 17

It turned out that plenty of people had gone in and out of
the Royal Arms during the hours our team had been situated
outside. Our eyes on the doors of the run-down, single room
occupancy hotel reported a steady flow of people coming and
going, with none of them being—or even resembling—Mann.
They were confident that he was still inside.

I found that cold comfort. Probably because Falcon was
taking perverse pride in HU's skill by listening in on the chatter regarding my escape from the office building in Heartcore.
When I considered that our Heartcore brethren were still la-
boring under the assumption that I was somehow hiding inside
it gave me a distinctly uncomfortable feeling. After all, what
they missed, we could as well.

Rabino's check of the building went smoothly. His contact
at the planning office didn't identify any weaknesses that we
couldn't keep our eyes on. The front door, back alley, and the
escape which ran down the front of the hotel were the exits.

Still, there was always the disguise angle. Having just fooled
a good chunk of New Dagonia's finest, I wasn't feeling particularly invincible. So I was the one who suggested we have
another peek inside.

That set off a flurry of activity designed to give me as much
safety as we could manage. Including the incredibly uncomfortable low profile vest I'd slipped on under my shirt, as well
as the scryer the team would be monitoring me on.

After all, a link is too big to hide from trained observation,
even the small ones detectives carry. They're not designed to

be left on, either. Fortunately Rabbit had packed one of the newest models, so I'd be able to receive chatter.

We'd spent a few minutes in the back of the lorry getting set up. "You're sure that you want to go in there?" asked Rabino quietly as he helped me back into my jacket. It was the third time he'd posed the question.

"I'm good, Prey, just a tourist looking for a flop."

"If Mann makes you, and he's got company...."

I nodded. The results were unlikely to be pleasant in that case, but the rest of the squad wasn't very casually attired, and our support team's charcoal uniforms would attract all the wrong kind of attention.

So, despite the humor Rabino had tried to inject into my attire, the truth was evident; even sticking out like as I did, I made a better candidate for an undercover plant than anyone else we had on hand. That meant going in and having a peek.

"He won't." I said it to reassure someone. Whether it was Rabbit, or myself, I'm not sure. "He was a long way down the street when I fired on the embassy. Besides, if the Heartcore units couldn't get a good look at me, I'm not worried about Mann."

"Trawler is going to kill us if we lose you."

"Good. Incentive to keep me alive."

"You're pretty good at doing that yourself." He shook his head. "Not trying to pry. You know I wouldn't. But how are you?"

"I feel fine. Can't explain the details because I don't even understand them, but I'm fine. Really."

"I'm not talking about that." He shuddered briefly. "Yeah, that part creeps me out, no offense."

"None taken."

"But I mean with Thief. With it being his last day."

I looked down at him. Rabino is smaller than the rest of us, but he's quicker with devices and thinks on his feet like few cops I've ever known. Can't dress himself to save his life, and his new girlfriend has no better taste, but he's got a good heart.

Maybe the best in HU, and not just on the primeshift squad. All I saw when I searched his eyes was worry.

"Everyone has to go sometime." I shrugged. "Two and a half decades of his life for the NDPD, and look at him."

"Yeah, he looks like crap. It's true." He pointed at me. "But you're not at all yourself lately. Last couple weeks you've been off. Something is *not* right."

"Stress."

"If you need to talk...."

"Sure, maybe sometime."

He sighed. "Well, I offered. But just remember, you've got a squad still. You're part of the unit."

I nodded and felt a brief burst of shame at the obviousness of my moping around. I glanced over at Thief and Falcon. The two were supposed to be talking over contingencies. Hargold looked beat. He looked a decade older after just five days.

"Aye, thanks, Rabbit." I hopped down out of the back of the lorry and wandered over towards my partner. He looked up and gave me a nod. Falcon smiled. "We all ready to do this?"

"Just finished off the last of the 'what if Griff fucks it all up' plans," said Bird.

"Comforting to know."

"You won't be making any mistakes, Griffon." Thief's eyes bored into my skull. "I haven't lost a partner in my career. So I'm not losing one tonight."

"I can handle Mann," I said, tapping my vest. "Besides, he won't make me."

"Not Mann we're that worried about," said Rabino as he joined the circle. "We still don't know anything about how much power he actually has. Makes it impossible to know what assets might be in play."

"Watch your ass," said Thief.

"I trust you'll be watching my assets for me," I said and flashed him a smile.

He held my eyes with his gaze for a moment and grunted. "We will. You can count on it." His tone left no doubt in my mind. My partner meant that *he* would have my back.

I almost shed a tear.

"Right then, lads," I said, smiling broadly to cover up the other rush of emotion. "Shall we switch me on, patch me in, and get this foolish plan underway?"

Less than two minutes later—right at 4:10PM, according to my chrono—I was walking in the front doors of the Royal Arms. The broad portals swung open with relative ease, revealing a ratty lobby in desperate need of a paint job. I wandered past the bank of clarions and headed into the lobby proper, wondering just how bad a mess I could be walking into.

I was still busy contemplating just how foolish the plan could possibly be when I spotted Lannik Mann coming down the stairs, and he wasn't alone.

I checked my stride for just a moment to keep a pillar between us for half a second as I recovered from the surprise. As I came back into his sight Mann looked right at me.

My breath caught in my throat for a moment before I was able to master my breathing. I forced myself to look away as nonchalantly as possible, and kept walking towards the front desk.

There were three other men with him. All of them were well-dressed, or at least expensively-dressed. I wasn't big on the colors the largest of the three was sporting. They made him look washed-out.

Each seemed wary enough, so I walked right past them and waved to the clerk behind the desk. For this job I broke out my native highland brogue and asked how his day was going. The man puzzled at the sound, but rose to help me. I heard the quartet wander on by behind me.

I kept on for a moment, asking about a room, but my mind was on other things. After the clerk named a price, I agreed, then asked him if he knew anything about the style of the pillars. I turned and took a look at the progress the four men were making under the guise of pointing out the decaying supports.

A carry pulled up outside just as I swung full about.

The four men kept walking towards the exit and I kept talking about the architecture of the dump. The clerk kept trying to interject, but I prattled on. First complimenting the lines of the ceiling, then asking if the owner might not want to clean it up a bit. Also, was that urine I smelled?

As my targets cleared the door and it swung shut, I canned the burr and slipped back into my adopted accent. I flipped my sigil open behind me and let it flare. "NDPD. Shut up." The clerk stopped talking immediately. I slapped the case closed again as I rattled off information to my team.

"Mann is on the move. He's in a late model Kandry. Looks like maybe a Raven. Dark blue, I do not—I repeat, do not—have a number, but it's pulling away from the entrance now."

"We have a visual," said Sergeant Ulman.

"He has four companions. The three with him look like muscle. One like not much more than muscle. Didn't see the driver."

"Keep your distance," said Thief. "Bird-n-Prey, trade off surveillance with Ulman. Shadow only. Let's see where they're headed."

"You got it," Falcon said. I could almost see the grin on his face.

"We're westbound, one block behind," said Ulman.

"On your six, half a block back," said Bird.

"Can I get a pick up?" I asked.

"Oh, aye, laddie," said Thief in his best—or worst, I can never tell with any of the squad—Kaledonian accent. "Be right around."

I groaned and walked towards the doors.

I hadn't missed my guess at the carry's profile. Mann and company's vehicle was in fact a Kandry Raven. Shiny and new, at that. The number on the plate wasn't present; a dealer's temporary tearaway sheet in the back window served as identification instead.

Rabino had run the Raven and tracked it to a dealership in Timberhold. The vehicle had been purchased in cash just an hour earlier.

Whatever the communication had been, it was clear that Mann had somehow triggered an escape contingency. If the clean vehicle wasn't a big enough clue, the fact that a trip through the Sunset Gate ward ended with the carry exiting the city through the magnificent portal.

Once we were outside the city proper, Thief and I took over the tail from Ulman and his partner. Hargold had the marked units slide back into the steadily thinning rush hour traffic. They kept close enough to get to us in case of trouble—probably, at least—but far enough back they wouldn't bother Lannik or his associates.

Homicide Unit doesn't leave the walls too often. Not as many murders out in the provincial regions, and the local detectives tend to handle most of the crime that does crop up. We get the occasional call still, but mainly we stick to the city proper; or The Liberties, the anachronistically-named suburban creep situated outside the gates.

But I'd spent plenty of time training with the NDA outside the sprawl. So when we finally managed to clear the ever-expanding ring of development I actually started to feel strangely at home. New Dagonia is much more arid than Kaledon, but nature is nature, and the provincial regions are full of unsullied—or perhaps, just less-sullied—natural beauty.

New Dagonia's borders afford those seeking exodus a quicker path to the east than the north, and the western route is long and winding. The mountains which form the natural and political border aren't terribly forgiving terrain. Yet as the evening grew longer and the light threatened to dim, Mann and his friends worked their way doggedly west into the rising foothills which led to the Amilar border crossing.

I tapped on the console and sighed as I checked my chrono. 7:54PM. "You know we have to stop them soon, right?"

Thief grunted. "Yeah." He slid past Falcon's unit and stared the tail of the Raven which was three carries ahead of us and a lane over to the right.

"We've got nothing on him."

"Mann is guilty." He paused for a moment then sighed. "But I know we have no evidence."

"How's this going to go?"

He shrugged. "To be honest, Griff, I've not got a fucking clue. I wanted dispatch to call with some last second news from DMU. Some oddity to match to Mann." He pointed at the unit's link and frowned. "This thing seems awfully quiet to me."

"Aye."

"What if we take him in?"

"There's the chance we'd get outed for pushing him around this afternoon. But we could sit on him a couple days."

"You could."

"Aye." I shook my head. "But I know you want him, and you want him today. So how do we get him?"

"I don't know. I'd like to keep him in the country though. Amilar would get cranky if we touched him after we cross over." We passed another sign counting down the miles to the border. Less than an hour and we'd be there, even with the slow climb into the mountains proper which we were about to start.

"We really only have a few options. None of them are good." I paused and considered. "A couple of them are very illegal."

"Start listing them," he said as he adjusted his position behind the wheel and stretched.

"Any order you like?"

"Start with the least likely to get the entire primeshift squad fired all at once. I only have so much couch space."

I pointed ahead of us at the Raven. The vehicle started to slow and turn into the first of a series of wide switchbacks. "We stop them and take Mann in for questioning. Either he breaks, or DMU finds something to link him to Murder."

"He won't break."

"No, he won't. If DMU was going to swoop in and save us, they probably would have already. I suspect you got the best detectives you could assigned to that warrant." He nodded, and I held up a pair of fingers. "We stop them, and we break him down out here."

"Might be a hard sell in court when he denies anything ever happened and has all his buddies back him up." He paused, then turned towards me. "Hey, Griff, you don't suppose we could get—"

"No." I shook my head firmly. Hargold was asking if my ex-girlfriend might take the case. He could want this guy more than anything in the world, but I was not going to deal with asking Cora for anything. Besides, it wouldn't work. "She's retiring soon. So even if she asked, she'd never be assigned the case."

"She'd do it for you."

"Oh I doubt that." There was no way I'd put myself in that position.

"Looked in a mirror lately?"

"Green eyes and good teeth don't make up for my failings." Or make me crazy enough to get into that kind of toxic relationship again.

"I wish I had your teeth."

"Thanks." I sighed. "Last idea is the worst one."

"I figured." I could hear tension, and his posture was braced. As if white-knuckling the wheel would make the news less unpleasant.

"It's really bad." He made no comment, so I kept going. "We take him, and his men, and we provoke a fight."

"We don't know they're armed."

"I'm more worried about the fact that we don't know they're not."

"Are five men really going to take on eight NDPD officers? They're going to know we can't just kill them. They'll come quietly and—"

"Wait," I said, cutting him off. "They will, and that's perfect."

"How is it perfect? We get five guys, four we don't want, and nobody talking about anything but the vacation we ruined when we brought them in."

"We get five guys, yeah. How are we going to transport five of them?"

"We've got plenty of room—"

"Not in one carry."

He opened his mouth, then shut it again. "We just happen to take Mann."

I nodded. "His friends happen to end up in other carries."

"And then it's just the three of us."

"Aye."

"Griff, are you...." He trailed off and looked at me.

I shook my head. "Do you even have to ask that?"

Thief smiled, just a slight bit. But it was more than I'd seen in a while. I picked up the link and started calling in the cavalry.

CHAPTER 19

We hit them just fifteen minutes shy of the Amilar crossing. After alerting the others of the plan, we'd crept forward and managed to pass Mann and his companions. There was a tense moment when we slid by, but the driver didn't blink, and the others looked as if they were in deep conversation over something exciting.

Safely past, Hargold and I cruised along in the line of cars headed for a weekend out of the country and waited for the rest of the team. We were just one more carriage in a column filled with friends, co-workers, and couples looking forward to enjoying the hospitality of New Dagonia's neighbor. Most were no doubt headed to the famed boardwalks of seaside favorites Taniston and Yarlow. The gambling, dining, and shows were a steady draw.

A couple of minutes passed as the others maneuvered into position. After getting the final report back from Ulman's partner, I gave the word. In an instant, the Kandry we'd shadowed from the city was boxed in my NDPD carriages. Lights blazing; sirens howling. We guided our quarry firmly into one of the long turnouts used by the stream of slow-moving lorries which made the steep climb every day. Hargold slowed steadily and brought us to rest with the Raven a few dozen yards behind us.

"Ready?" Thief asked as he set the parking brake.

"Am I ever not?" I asked. I said it in my best, most cheerful tone, but I knew the lie for what it was. After as many years as we'd been together, Hargold probably did as well.

I was exhausted. The week had run me down, and whatever the overwhelmingly positive physical effects of the spell I'd managed, there seemed to be a payment due. Even the spirit was resting. Fitfully, perhaps, but it wasn't crouched in wait like I'd come to expect from potential confrontations.

Still, I popped my door and stepped out of the Hallowstone. The gravel of the shoulder was rough beneath my feet. I wiggled my shoes in it for a moment and stretched.

"Coming?"

"Aye. Just enjoying being upright."

"I suppose they can sweat," said Thief. He yawned and arched his back, throwing his arms out wide. I glanced at the others and they were all doing the same. Except for Ulman. He was staring right at the Raven, hand resting on his service wand, with a half-smile on his face.

"Right then," I said, straightening my jacket and smoothing out my kilt. "Shall we?"

We approached the carry slowly. By the time we were halfway there, every member of the team had eyes on the vehicle. None of the men inside it were moving.

Thief stopped next to the Raven and made a motion to the driver. The window lowered. "Hi there," he said, briefly flashing his sigil. "Nice carry. Where'd you get it?"

The driver was young. Maybe twenty. Probably not yet. He didn't answer. It was the big, tough-looking fellow with poor taste who spoke up from the seat next to the kid. "I bought it this afternoon."

"Oh yeah? You get a good deal?"

"It was ok," he said, eyes narrowing. "Why do you ask?"

"Been looking at one. I'm retiring today, and I'll need a new ride once I turn that baby in." He pointed at the Hallowstone and smiled. "Fast damn carry, that. Tough too. Thought maybe a Raven. My partner's Sparrow lasted forever." He nodded at me.

"Damn fine carries." I said. "Can't go wrong with a Kandry."

"So which dealer was it? I only ask because we got this call from the Kandry dealership in Timberhold. Apparently some-one dropped a bunch of counterfeit liri on a Raven and drove it away before the floor manager noticed."

"That's a fucking lie!" the heavy man shouted.

"Easy," said Mann from the back.

"He's fucking lying. I wouldn't screw up like—"

"Shut up," said Mann. The big man clamped his jaw shut and glared at Thief.

"I'm afraid I'm going to need to ask you to step out of the vehicle," said my partner as he took a step back. "One at a time, if you please."

"Not you," I said, pointing at the brooding muscle who had started to move for his door handle. "Driver first, please."

Thief pointed the young man at Falcon and Rabino. The youth walked towards our squadmates slowly, checking over his shoulder every few steps. Bird-n-Prey led him to the back of their Hallowstone, did a cursory frisk, and pushed him in.

"Now, can I have the next...there, you, go on and get out. Walk over to the officers waving to you." One of Mann's two backseat companions—a man with eyes just a bit too close to-gether—was received by the second patrol unit. "And next up is you, big guy." Thief pointed to Ulman, who grinned. "Go see the nice Sergeant."

The look the big man gave Thief could have curdled milk fresh from the cow. I was happy the monstrosity wasn't ours to deal with.

"I'll take this one," I said, motioning to Mann. "Maybe send the last one over to—"

"Yeah, yeah, kid looks worried. Why don't you go hang out with your little buddy?" asked Thief as I led Mann away. "You know, we detectives have the comfy rides anyway."

"Better than a blue and white," I called over my shoulder.

"Less conspicuous too," said Thief.

I walked the last twenty paces to Hargold's unit silently. Mann didn't turn around, just kept on going at a steady, re-laxed pace.

"Here we go, sir," I said to Mann, smiling. I turned him up against the vehicle and relieved him of his keys when I found them. I left the wallet and coin purse in his pockets without checking them. I didn't even touch his chrono. "Now, I have to take these keys since they're a potential weapon. The rest you can keep. Regulations, you know." I opened the door. "If you'll just do me a favor and sit down in the back here?"

He did as I asked, then glared up at me. "You think I don't recognize you? That I'm some kind of idiot?"

"Hmm?"

"How many morons wear a damned kilt as a disguise?"

"You don't like? These are my new clothes. Not my usual style, I'll admit, but that's a long story."

"I saw you at the hotel," he said.

"Funny, I saw you there too." I rattled my shackles in my hand. "Put these on please. Can't have you loose. Against regulations in a detective's unit."

"This isn't about counterfeiting, or the Raven."

"You're saying that the NDPD would have a reason to detain your party other than the vehicle which was reported stolen, and the counterfeit goods which were passed off during that transaction? What would that be?"

Lannik set his jaw and narrowed his eyes. "That incident you're referring to? That never happened."

"He resisting the shackles, Griff?" asked Thief as he returned to the carry. The menace in his voice was barely concealed.

"Hasn't seen fit to wear them as of yet," I said, shaking them again.

Thief shook his head and smiled. "Come on, Mann, it won't kill you."

"See, you even know my name!" Lannik looked angry. "And you look familiar too," he said, staring at my partner.

"What?" Thief rubbed his head.

"His name," I said to my partner. "Your name?" I asked, tilting my head at the killer.

Our detainee screwed up his face and turned red. "Mann!"

"Huh, funny, his name *is* Mann." I gave him a chuckle. "What do you figure his last name is?"

"That is my last name."

Thief laughed; not a pleasant noise. "Hilarious." He wiped the mirth from his face in a second. "Put the shackles on. Right now."

I shrugged and nodded. "Regulations. You can wear them up front though." I gave him a thin smile. "Since you're just being detained. For now."

Mann put the shackles on and I checked them. "I'm wearing them," he said.

"Regulations," I said with a smile. Then I slammed the door on him and banished the expression.

CHAPTER 20

"Where are we going?" asked Mann. He sounded confused. Not surprising considering the rest of our unit had just made the turn to head back towards the city. Thief kept driving west into the setting sun.

I turned in my seat. "What's it matter? You don't have anywhere to be."

"The other officers—"

"They've gone and headed back to New Dagonia."

"Where are *we* headed?"

Thief reached over and killed the recording devices. He looked at me and nodded. We were past the point of no return.

"Lannik Mann, you have been a very bad boy," said my partner. The killer's eyes flew open and he recoiled.

"So shocked, Mann?" I shook my head. "Five days ago you committed a heinous crime on our watch. Did you think we wouldn't find you?"

"I don't know what you're talking about."

"Doesn't matter. See, normally we get the call on a body and it's a sad happening, but we deal. Part of the Job. Do our best to find criminals, put them away. Sometimes it works, and sometimes it doesn't."

"Normally," Thief said.

"This wasn't just another nobody you killed." Something flickered across Mann's face in the fading light. "This happened to be an acquaintance of my partner here."

"Murder and I went way back. All the way back, if you know what I mean."

Mann had started to sweat. "What are y—"

Thief scoffed. "Come on, Mann. You know his name."

"Gallan Armos," I said. "Born Gallan Murder, in Green-fields. Nasty place, I hear. Or it was, before they shut it down for being too nasty."

"To be fair—as someone who knows—nasty doesn't do it justice. Awful place to grow up. As one of the kids in there, well, if you made a true friend it was like having a brother."

Mann held up his shackled hands and gave the best shrug he could. "You have the wrong—"

"No," I said. "No, we don't." I pointed across the road at an upcoming break in the barriers, and a small sign. "There's the turnoff."

"Got it," said Thief.

"Where are we going?" asked Lannik. His hands were linked together now, and they looked to be shaking a bit.

"End of the fucking line is where," said Thief.

"See, Mann, your mistake wasn't one you could have avoid-ed," I said. "There was no way you could've known Gallan was friends with the lead detective of the NDPD Homicide Unit." Thief pulled across the lanes as he spotted a break in traffic. Then he turned down the dirt road away from the highway, winding across the mountainside.

I gestured out the window at the view. It was impressive. "You wanted to escape New Dagonia, Mann?" I pointed west towards Amilar. "You're going to."

"You can't do this! You're cops!" Spittle flew from his lips as he shouted it.

"You're an agent of what effectively amounts to a faction of a foreign government."

"I'm a citizen of New Dagonia!" His response wasn't much more than a squeak by the end.

Thief laughed. "You're a spy and a killer. And before I was a cop, I was CID."

I jerked my head to look at him. His face showed nothing, but I was nearly sure he wasn't kidding.

All the years working with him, and I'd had no clue.

Counter Intelligence Division was the agency assigned to investigation and prevention of all domestic espionage. Spy hunters and cell breakers. They didn't do a lot of walking around announcing themselves, and penalties for foreign agents were swift and permanent. They could be very quiet as well, when necessary.

"I'm not a spy!"

"You're a member of a Salleean syndicate," said Thief. "Close enough for me."

Mann stared at me. I shrugged. "I just don't like you. I've got a hole in my favorite duster because of this case."

"He really loves that coat."

"You can't...," Mann whimpered for a while after that.

We slowed, then stopped. Hargold and I stepped out of the carriage, into the brilliance of the sunset. Amilar was laid out in all its glory, down through the valleys, into the foothills and across the rolling, open plains that dominated the country. We could see the shore to the southwest, and what looked like the lights of the boardwalks a bit further in.

Mann sat in the Hallowstone for a minute, gibbering and snotting on himself. It didn't really affect my enjoyment of the view. It was the most magnificent of sunsets. Better than I'd seen in years.

Hargold leaned against the front of the Hallowstone and looked out at the sights. He seemed old. Almost brittle. Nothing like the man who had taken me under his wing and brought me into the NDPD.

"I'm with you," I said. "To the end." He looked up and nodded.

I walked around and opened up the rear door. "Time to go," I said. Mann thrashed and backed away from me.

And fell out the door Thief opened behind him.

The air was knocked out of him by the fall, so we hauled him to his feet. The murderer staggered along between us for a moment before starting to struggle again.

I tightened my grip on his arm as Mann struggled. We dragged him closer to the drop-off. Closer to the border. Closer to justice.

"Goodbye, you piece of shit," said Thief as we reached the small wooden fence which separated us from the edge of the precipice.

Our captive looked over the edge and howled.

CHAPTER 21

Mann broke the noise off after a few seconds and started to babble, rapid-fire. "Stop. Just stop. And I—I'll confess. I'll sign. I'll do anything. Anything. Stop. Please. Please." By the end his words were choked off, barely more than a whisper. He was shaking.

Right then is when I smelled the urine mixed with feces.

I stepped back just a bit, but kept my grip and forced him towards the fence. "Only one way to deal with you now, Lannik. That's a short trip down to Amilar." I jerked him closer the the barrier. "They'll probably never even find you in the ravine over there. The animals will get you. Elements will wash all the traces away."

"No! Listen...I killed him. I shot him. Twice—"

"That's it—" I hauled on his arm, bringing him to the fence itself.

He struggled and shouted. "In th—the chest! On—once in the head!"

"How original," said Thief as he dragged the other half of Mann's body to the edge. He wedged the struggling man up against the wooden barrier. "Like nobody's ever seen that before on the tapestry. Three times a night on some fucking bullshit cop drama. Make up some more stories why don't you."

Mann started crying again. Between his sobs and sniffles he spilled information.

He talked about the cheap ice wand he'd acquired in Black Spit the night of the murder. How the dealer had assured him that the weapon was fresh off the boat from who-knows-where with no paper trail to cause trouble. He told us about where Murder was in the apartment, and how two blasts from the wand had taken him down. About the third he'd triggered while standing over the fallen man. He'd struck Murder in the brow with the final discharge.

He had started to calm down as he talked, so we pulled him back from the edge.

"Sit," said Thief. He kicked the murderer's legs out from under him. Mann went down hard and cracked his head against one of the posts.

"Why did you kill him?" I asked. "And please, when answering, recall that only our curiosity is keeping your worthless ass alive right now. Don't abuse our sensibilities with lies."

Thief nodded from where he loomed over Lannik. "Do that, you little prick, and I'll enjoy a cigar while watching the sun set over your corpse."

"I swear, I'll tell you the truth," said the killer. "Don't kill me, just—"

"Doesn't sound too interesting." Thief reached down for Mann's arm.

"Wait!" He shrunk away from my partner. "Wait...just a second."

"Did my friend beg for his fucking life, you piece of garbage? Did he ask you to stop? Did you even say a word before you killed him?"

"Answer his questions," I said.

"I let myself in."

"How?"

"We own the buildings. We have all the keys." He licked his lips. "I walked in. He was sitting down, but got up when he saw me. I shot him to keep him quiet, but he made a lot of noise going down. I finished him off right away. He didn't suffer."

I glanced over the fence. "You probably won't either."

Thief shrugged. "Unless he gets *lucky*...and survives the fall."

"I'm telling you what you want!" Mann's whole body shook.

"Just take me in."

"You didn't answer his question," Hargold said as he nodded at me.

"What?"

"No, *why.*"

"Oh, yeah, yeah, sorry, sorry." He swallowed hard and tried to calm himself. He stopped shaking as much and spit out the story. "It's all because of the robbery."

"The one where you stole from secured storage," I said. "Stole something that belonged to Tandem."

"Yeah. It's complicated."

"Well, *we* still have plenty of time to live."

"Fuck. Fuck. You guys are cops."

"We're also people, with feelings, and you've upset my partner."

Thief growled.

"Shit, ok, look," said Mann. "I was given the job, my first job for the Carsibal syndicate, to get some fucking illuminations, all right?"

"Illuminations." I shook my head. "What kind of illuminations?"

"Blackmail kind. Extortion. The kind of illuminations that turn over the reins of a syndicate from one heavy hitter to another."

"It was an internal power struggle?"

"Yeah. Only I made a mistake, and someone died. Your friend didn't like that. Because it could have been him, or because they knew each other. Maybe both...I don't know."

"But you paid him off," said Thief. "Got him to like it with a bribe. What was he threatening to do?"

"He was going to the cops, said he knew someone. 'A new recruit,' is how he said it. Someone he could trust, and who'd believe him.

"Maybe you?" I asked

Thief shrugged. "Maybe." Then he nodded. "All right, probably. The timing fits, but with his past I wasn't the only cop

Murder knew."

Mann kept going. "He got money. He got a place to live, but he didn't know about that part. I got him a couple of places by steering him in the right direction."

"Places Tandem owned," I said.

"Yes."

"To spy on him." Thief jerked his head at Lannik. "See, I knew I smelled a spy"

"I had to be sure he wasn't going to back out. My boss ordered it."

"Did your boss order the hit?"

Mann stayed quiet for a moment. "You have to understand—"

"No, I don't." Thief hauled him upright and shoved him at the fence. Mann started to topple over and screamed. My partner caught his shackles and half shouted the question. "Did your boss order his fucking execution, or not?"

"Yes, yes!" The murderer's feet slid and shifted in the dirt. The wood bent under his weight and threatened to give way. "Gallan was playing a fucking event in Sallee. He spotted the old boss. The guy in the illuminations. He fucking *talked*."

Thief hauled on the shackles and shoved Lannik to the ground. "What did he say?"

"I don't know. Just, well, the guy never knew who was blackmailing him, but Murder knew too much. He knew me. He knew Jasyn really well, he—"

"Jasyn?" I asked.

"Yeah."

"Who is that?"

"Oh, sorry, I thought you knew. The third guy in our crew. The one that got killed."

"No ID was ever made. All we had was a dead body, and a sketch of Murder they never connected to anybody."

Thief nodded. "Until you recognized it."

"Whoever saw him got the eyes right." I prodded Mann with my toe. "Keep going, wanker. What did he know?"

"My boss. He knew my boss. Stupid fucking mistake, right? Meeting with hired help? I told him I could handle things, but no, he wanted to know about this B&E expert I'd found. Interviewed Gallan him-fucking-self."

"You don't think much of the boss then."

"Not *the* boss, just my boss. He didn't take over the Carsibal, just got a better paying position when the new head reorganized."

"Still, not a fan."

"He's arrogant and takes too many risks, but he gave me control of Tandem and put me in charge of all the syndicate's interests in New Dagonia."

"So your boss—whose name you are about to give us...." Mann stared at the dirt. I continued. "Who is a right bastard when you think about it, seeing as how you're hung the fuck out to die right about now."

"You can't touch him, he's in Sallee."

"Oh, Mann," said Thief. "What we do with the information is up to us. What you need to do is fucking give it up, or I start breaking your fucking bones *before* you go over the edge."

"I've told you what you wanted to know! Take me back in! I swear I'll confess. I swe—"

"You swear now while your dick is in the wind and the last sunset you'll ever see is just about to fade away," I said and waved a hand across the glorious panorama. "Turn your head and look, Lannik. You're going to want to hold onto this memory for however many seconds you have left."

His eyes flicked towards the fading bands of red, pink, and purple. He started to cry a little more. Quietly this time. "Then why should I tell you?" he asked as he turned back towards me.

"I believe my partner made it clear what happens if you don't. If it were me I'd go as painlessly as possible."

Which was a complete lie, of course. I'd have taken my chances fighting long before being dangled over a cliff. But Mann was a behind-the-scenes guy at heart. A chatterbox. Aye, he got his hands dirty sometimes. But only when the odds were stacked in his favor.

"I'll start with your fingers," said Thief.

"Tanthir Ariscomb is one of the captains in the Carisbal. Before the Tandem job he was just muscle with aspirations. Afterward he became much, much more powerful. He's gotten the Carisbal's fingers into dozens of the countries in this region."

"So he's powerful enough that when he said you needed to personally kill my friend, even your coward self had to obey."

"Yes."

"That's all I needed to know," said Thief as he drew his wand. I stepped back away from Mann, whose jaw dropped.

"I told you everything," he said in a piteous voice.

"You did. You also killed my friend. Because your fucking boss got his dick caught in the wringer, you cleaned up an inconvenience."

"Wait...."

"I'm going to clean up an inconvenience now, you piece of shit." Thief raised his wand.

I watched as he activated it, and I didn't even blink when the blast struck.

CHAPTER 22

Monday morning wasn't anything like I'd thought it would be.

I'd found myself sitting in the bull pen earlier than usual. No real reason for it; other than the decision to stop chasing the sleep which had eluded me.

Coffee on the way in hadn't lasted, so I'd been making do with the brew from the brand new pot. Tasted about the same as the old one.

I sat and stared at Thief's empty desk as the minutes ticked away to roll call. The chair he'd occupied for all the years of our partnership seemed lonely. I was tempted it bring it a cup of coffee, but decided against. People would be showing up soon, and I didn't want to look too crazy.

Even though I felt like I was.

"Dire," said Captain Trawler from the far side of the bull pen. I looked up, and he beckoned. "Come to my office."

I grabbed my coffee and walked through the aisle to the break in the partition leading to the dwarf's domain. I paused and looked back to see if Hargold was coming. Of course not. Just an empty chair at the desk he'd cleared out early Saturday morning.

Trawler was waiting just inside the office. He motioned to the chairs in front of his desk and I picked one out. "How was your weekend?" he asked, closing the door.

"Started off better than it ended."

The Captain crossed behind his massive desk and hopped up onto the tall-backed chair. "You all must have been very busy with the paperwork."

"That wasn't so bad."

The truth of it was that we'd had an incredible amount of reporting to do. Thief, Falcon, Rabino and myself had worked through until Saturday afternoon tying things up. I hadn't minded a bit. It was a stay of execution, no matter how brief.

But the end rolled around. Thief called in off duty for the last time just after he finished boxing up his desk. I'd checked my chrono out of habit, and he'd given me a huge smile. Never said why, exactly; but he'd been happy, and he'd looked like death.

Afterward we'd driven back to his place, had a couple of drinks, and then he'd kicked me out as midnight drew closer. My drive home had gotten me back just in time to watch Sunday roll around; a day I'd spent on whisky and memories.

Trawler smiled at me and rubbed his well-trimmed beard. "I've only started to get into it, but a couple of reports were shoved on the top of the pile."

"You had questions? Were they my accounts?"

He shook his head. "No, not really." The dwarf was silent for a few moments. "I'm reassigning you to desk duty—"

"Captain! I—"

"—temporarily! Just for a while, Griffon."

"Why?"

"All three of your squadmates filled a report specifically citing your recklessness." He scratched the back of his head. "Funny thing is, Dire, none of them will say exactly what happened that concerned them."

I shrugged. "I don't know...but Cap—"

"No. It's done. You're assigned to your desk for now. I'll reevaluate in two weeks, but I don't promise to let you back onto the streets even then."

I pushed to my feet and leaned on the desk. Being solidly over six feet tall gave me a towering presence compared to a seated dwarf, even a giant like Trawler. "Where do you get off shackling me to the desk? I'm a thrice-damned fine detective.

I get results."

Trawler looked up at me and met my eyes. His stony face was impassive; hard gray eyes unwavering. "You do. That's indisputable. And I want you to be around to keep getting those results. I'll get nothing from a corpse."

"Fuck you, Captain."

"Sorry, Griffon, but no." He shrugged. "What can I say? My wife would kill me if I accepted your offer."

"You're a complete bloody wanker, Argo."

"Comes with the rank, kid. Now, sit the fuck down." I did. "Better. I'm going to leave you with one last thought: consider what you want to do now that Thief is retired."

"What I want to do?" I wrinkled my brow and frowned. "What's that supposed to mean?"

"It means you're a detective without a partner, and you have some options available to you." He shrugged. "Other units need good cops too, Dire."

"I want to stay in HU."

"All I'm saying is to consider your options."

"Fine."

"That's it. Go on."

I pushed myself upright and stormed out.

CHAPTER 23

"**G**o fuck yourself you manky, thrice-damned wanker," I said under my breath as I walked with purpose towards the stairs. My face felt hot. My pulse hammered in my throat. It was difficult to breathe.

So I ran the steps to the parapet. Faster than usual, and with a bit more abandon than was strictly called for given that they were well-trafficked, even before primeshift. I almost knocked over a couple of uniforms between the seventh and eighth floor.

When I reached the top of the tower my first order of business was to find a quiet spot. That meant settling for a seat on the north side, away from the view of the Yarin.

Which was fine, really. I didn't need to watch the boats on the river. I needed to calm down.

So I stared out at the city. Then I cast my gaze to the west and stared at the road leading away from the city, off towards the mountains.

I was still staring at them when my squadmates found me.

"Hey," said Rabino as he hopped up onto the wall beside me.

"Missed you at roll call," said Falcon. He leaned up against the barrier on the other side of me.

"Didn't feel like it," I said.

"No doubt. Sorry."

"Why, Kif?"

"Thief made us," said Rabbit. "You scared him to death, and he's terrified of what you're going to be like now that he's gone. Frankly, so am I."

"Add me to that worry party," said Bird.

There were a few minutes of silence which followed their admissions. I chewed the bitter pills. They left well enough alone.

I broke the silence when I was ready. "You stay the night with him?" I asked Rabino.

"Yeah." He drummed his fingers on the top of the wall. "He'll walk again. With therapy."

"Thief should have just killed him," said Falcon. "You wouldn't have ever said a word."

I nodded. When Hargold had put that blast through Mann's leg I hadn't even felt an ounce of remorse at being complicit in the assault. As the killer had rolled on the ground in his own shit, piss, and blood, I'd felt nothing more than satisfaction.

"He did the right thing," said Rabino.

"How so?" I was mostly surprised because of the four of us— or perhaps the three of us, now that Thief was gone—Rabbit had always been the most beholden to the regs.

"He didn't kill Mann. That's worth something, at least."

"Aye, he let the bastard live. Put the fear into him though. I have the feeling Lannik got the message."

"What message?"

I grinned at Prey. "If he tries to do anything but plead guilty to the murder he's a dead man."

Rabino sighed. "Well, it's more than he did for Thief's friend. What chance did Armos have?"

"I half expected you to write the truth in your report."

He shrugged. "What would I have written? You told me he was shot trying to escape. I wasn't there."

"Thanks."

Bird smiled at his partner. "You're a fucking fine cop, Griff. It is an honor to serve with you. There's no way Rabbit would dick up our squad."

"Trawler wants to." I made a sour face.

"Let me guess?" he asked.

I nodded. "Aye, go ahead."

"The Captain says you need to take your time while on desk

duty and ponder a change of unit."

"Mmm, oh aye. Bastard. As if I want anything but HU."

"Look, I hear you." He pointed out across the city. "I live for this shit. We all do. But you just took a big hit. Thief was your other half for six years. You don't just shake that shit off in any case, and you guys were tighter than a maiden."

"I want HU."

"And HU wants you. But you can work the clarion and do some paperwork for a while. Think of it as proving you really want it if you'd like. Trawler sees you taking the desk assignment seriously and he'll give you whatever you want."

Rabbit nodded. "It's the truth. You can demand what you want, if you play along."

He was about to continue but stopped abruptly.

Falcon turned and both of them moved away. "Later, Griff," said the senior detective as they beat a retreat.

"I'm not ready to talk, Captain," I said as I turned around.

"Good," said Hargold. "I fucking hate chit chat."

My heart soared for a moment, then dropped out again. "Last little bits of admin, huh?"

He nodded. "Never-ending fucking paperwork, kid. All I want to do is get away from that shit, you know?"

"Pull up a chunk of wall," I said, motioning to the barrier.

"Sure thing."

We sat for over an hour; silently watching the metropolis go about its business.

Other officers came and went, smoking, chattering, laughing. Sometimes they would come and stand near us in their little clusters.

Mostly they steered clear, leaving us to our communion with the city.

Thief got down off the wall when the time was right. He did it slowly, deliberately, and the fatigue he was suffering from was clear as he did. The frailty the past week had awakened in him was probably temporary, but it hurt to see.

"Take care of her, Griff." He extended his hand.

I hopped off my own perch and took it. The warm, solid pressure of my ex-partner's grip was reassuring.

"You know I will."

"Of course." He looked around the parapet and shook his head. "Well, I'll be going then. Couple more pieces of paperwork for me to do."

"Aye. Wouldn't want you to miss getting that abundant pension."

"Wouldn't want that, no."

"Chime me this weekend," I said. He nodded and turned away.

I watched in silence as my partner of six years—and truly my best friend in all the Thousand Kingdoms—headed back inside the watchtower. After Thief disappeared I stared at the archway for a moment before shaking my head and turning back to the wall.

In my brief absence the sun had warmed my seat. I settled back in and turned my face up towards the warmth. I basked in it for a moment before I cast my eyes back across the sprawl.

For a brief, fanciful moment I wondered if the city could feel the loss of one of its fiercest protectors. Then I decided it was enough that I could.

Nobody came looking for me. Hours fell away, and I passed them in contemplation.

By the time I'd watched the sun set over the mountains I'd made my decision.

I wandered inside to go write Trawler a letter.

☆DEAD'S☆NIGHT

REFLECTIONS

*O*ften enough, the days which change our lives forever look a lot—on the face of them—like any other day. Sometimes the changes they work on us are so subtle we hardly realize that we've been fundamentally altered.

My first day at university was like that. So was the first kiss I shared with Raysa. It wasn't until years later, when I was in the Army, that I understood how my thoughts were different because of my education. *And* as for my first love—my only real love for so many years—it wasn't until she was buried that the 18-year-old me saw what our relationship had truly meant. How vital it had been to an orphan who'd already lost everything once, a decade earlier.

Then there are the other days. The ones which consist of events about as subtle as a wand stuck in your face by a desperate man. Times like those you know right then that you'll never look at your life the same way again. But even then—even knowing something is life-altering—you can miss just how big a change it really is. In the heat of the crucible you don't see what effect the trial will have.

So I can hardly be blamed for not seeing the latest turning point for what it truly was. It would take weeks before I even started to understand what that night—the night I risked everything, for no real reason—meant to my future. Even then, months would need to pass before the ramifications of what I'd set in motion that evening would become clear in my thoughts.

By then, as they say, it would be far too late to do anything about it.

CHAPTER 1

If there's one thing I miss about my life before joining the department, it's listening to music while driving. When I was still in the Army I would take my leave and drive my Sparrow just about anywhere I could, listening to whatever suited my mood best. But NDPD regs are strict about tuning in to the waves when on duty, and Detectives are almost always on duty when they're in their unit. My pool issue Hallowstone doesn't even have a tuner as a result.

So instead of the latest hits, or even something classic, I get to wait, watch the city go by, and listen for my link to tell me where the next body is. At least that's what I used to do. Not a lot of action for me recently. No action at all, to be exact.

The boredom of my forced penance has me *this* close to taking a holiday and just driving, listening, and watching the scenery flow by. At least then I'd have something in my ears again.

The sad fact is that silence—broken only by the carriage's crystal drive, the elements, and the sounds of the city—has become such a companion to my daily routine that the long-forgotten hissing precipitating a burst from the link is a surprise.

I startle at the noise and swerve, slipping just slightly out of my lane. A klaxon sounds to let me know I've irritated a fellow driver. My heart pounds as I bring the carry back on course.

"072707. Dispatch," says a woman's voice from across the void as my link sparks to life. "We have a patrol unit requesting backup in your vicinity. Can you assist?"

I growl. It's pissing down rain and I'm late for a big party at my Army buddy Durrin's place. It's also a full moon and, on top of that, it also happens to be Dead's Night.

"Dispatch. 072707," I say as I glance out the window of my Hallowstone at a crowd of masked revelers dancing around outside a pub, seemingly oblivious to the precipitation. "We have a corpse at that location?"

"Negative. Officers are requesting backup for a traffic stop. Possible stolen vehicle. No other units available in the vicinity."

I sigh. Of all the Holy Days, Dead's Night is unquestionably the single worst one for public servants like me. Arguably it's sacred to Akala. She of darkness. She who is faceless. She who greets the departed. Or, as I like to call her, she who is thrice-damned creepy. But the goddess' day has been taken over by pop culture in the past few decades.

Now it's an excuse to drink, masquerade, and generally cause problems. So it's a shit day of the year to be a cop—or, maybe even worse, a member of the Fire Brigade—in the City-State of New Dagonia. Even normal people become idiots when they dress up and drink too much. Even so, it wouldn't be so bad if accidents and mistakes were the worst of it.

But it's the fires that are the problem.

Every year there are more arson calls than the last. Gangs trying to prove their power. Kids trying to prove their fearless-ness. Pyromaniacs trying to prove they're better than all the amateurs.

So we all work overtime, and we answer the calls we can. Even when it means we're going to be later than late for our own celebrations.

"Send the route. I'm on my way."

"Incoming to your golem. Thank you, Detective." The link hisses eerily for a moment then goes silent.

I lean down and punch commands into the golem. It gets stuck for a minute and I have to reset it. The Hallowstone is aging, and slated for replacement. But since I'm only a second class I'll be waiting a while for a new unit.

Suits me fine. The Hallowstone is a beast of a carriage—at once more massive and faster than a patrol unit—and I love it. The new Barron carries are smaller and lighter. They can outmaneuver a Hallowstone to be sure, but they're not quite as fast. I'm happy to have my unit still.

I feel a little flutter of excitement as I wind my way through the streets of the Black Spit to the location. It's been months since Captain Trawler relegated me to desk duty. Six months. I haven't so much as flashed my sigil since my partner, Detective Thief, retired.

The Captain didn't take my wand and my sigil, but I've been doing all of the Homicide Unit paperwork, and none of the legwork. The prospect of a call—even one as simple as a vehicle stop—is an unexpected treat.

Minutes pass slowly as my stomach flutters, but I arrive at the stop without incident. As I pull in behind the patrol unit I make sure to flash my lights; just so nobody gets nervous. I kill the drive and step out of the carry into the rain.

First order of business is to grab my hat off the pile of clothes which constitute my festive garb for the party I'm missing. I pop the fedora on and wander back to my trunk. I quickly shrug out of my duster, then my jacket. Both of them land atop the earth rod as I grab my armor.

Vests are tight, stiff, and irritating. Plus they don't even stop all blasts. After my years in the NDA I'm far more comfortable in the type of armor worn by soldiers.

The hauberks worn by Rapid Response Unit officers are my style; they at least resemble the combat gear I trained with in the Army. But the vest is what we're issued as detectives. And—as much as I may hate it—I'm bloody sure I want to wear it right now.

After all, I'm in Black Spit—just blocks from the Warrens— and it's Dead's Night. I'd rather deal with the discomfort than end up at the Crypts, down on the Slabs, with Mari hovering over me.

I slip my jacket and duster back on. It takes me a minute to secure the coat completely, leg straps and all. But it's dumping buckets and I'm wet enough from the change. Almost as an afterthought, I grab my sigil out of the inner pocket of the duster.

"Detective?" asks a young uniform. He's timed his approach well, whether by accident or intent.

I smile at him, affix the sigil to my left breast pocket, and button back up. "Dire," I say through a curtain of rain only barely kept off my face by my lucky fedora.

"I'm Halbern," says the kid as I slam the trunk shut again. He looks like he's trying—in vain—to grow a mustache. "My partner is watching the vehicle. She's Stance."

We walk up to the driver's side of the blue and white. Stance is staring straight ahead, keeping track—as best she can through the downpour—of the activity in the carriage they've stopped. "Evening, Officer Stance," I say.

"Corporal."

"Sorry. Corporal Stance." I give her the respect she's looking for. Women have it hard in the NDPD. Lower advancement rate, less detective slots, and more desk jobs. Making Corporal as a woman isn't easy. "I'm Detective Dire, HU. What've you got?"

"The carry came up stolen when we ran the number. SOP is no unassisted stops of stolen vehicles."

"That a watchtower directive?"

"Yes. We don't do much alone in Black Spit, to be honest."

"I hear you." The ward wasn't one of the more common stops for me as a Homicide Unit detective. Not because people didn't die here, but because too many did. The Black Spit watchtower detectives handled most of them in house. Almost nobody important enough to have a thorough investigation into their death ever died in Black Spit.

When I come here on the Job it's usually running down someone with a grudge, or even a financial motive for seeing one of my victims in the ground.

"All right, Corporal." I tap on her door. "Let's see if we can't find out why this carriage popped up hot."

Stance steps out of the standard NDPD patrol car and slams

the angular door. I miss the Bluebird sometimes, but not as much as I'll miss the Hallowstone.

She jerks her head towards the low slung rear of the carriage. "Halbern, get the rod." I wonder if the order to grab the long arm is another directive. Probably just the intuition of a patrol officer with years of experience surviving in this ward.

The kid retrieves the rod and follows his partner with it at the ready. The three of us walk single file down the forty feet between the patrol unit and the carry of questionable origin.

The late model Tamm is a svelte roadster type I can't remember the name of. The driver has powered the drive down and parked it ten feet behind a small delivery lorry. The sporty carriage looks painfully out of place on the run-down streets of the poorest ward in New Dagonia. I figure the odds of it having been stolen from elsewhere in the city are very good indeed.

Maybe it's the carry that distracts me. Maybe I'm not as sharp as I was back in my own patrol days. Maybe bad things just happen on Dead's Night.

Whatever the case, I'm surprised when the attack begins.

CHAPTER 2

The first salvo of mixed elemental fire comes in as we're just over halfway to the carriage. Multiple projectiles strike Halbern. He drops like a stone into the water; silent, with a splash. He tumbles into a puddle and lies still.

I'm hit before I can react, but manage to roll with the impact, and the vest does its job. I'm raked by shards of earth from a rod. Other than being scraped up, I'm fine. The assault rouses my totem spirit, but I push it down as I crawl behind the Tamm, following the Corporal.

"Across the street," says Stance. I nod. We both pop up and take a quick peek. Through the driving rain I can see a half dozen masked individuals armed with wands and rods. Our attackers have arrayed themselves around the flower beds and benches which line the stairs leading up to a shopping arcade.

The incoming blasts have stopped. We haven't taken any since ducking behind the Tamm. I figure they know the thieves; why else bother holding fire?

I duck back behind cover and turn to look at Stance. As I open my mouth the Tamm's drive spins up. My heart sinks. "Move with it," I say in a low voice. "Get to cover behind that lorry and return fire."

The carry peels out and Stance runs with it. I get low and hustle back towards the blue and white. But not only do I have further to run than she does, I've got a stop to make out in no-man's-land.

I lock my hands around Halbern's arm as I move on by. I spin around backwards and start to haul for all I'm worth. The kid is lean, but he's close to my height, and his gear is added weight. Even dragging him without regard for his comfort, it's taking me far too long to get us into cover.

I hear Stance yelling, identifying us; as if they didn't see her uniform. I look up to see that she's started to return fire from her position behind the lorry. My estimation of her goes up a notch, and I find myself wondering if she's ex-military too.

But for Halbern and me the respite is brief. It's the Corporal's single service wand against many, and she's pinned back down within seconds. As Stance falls back into cover, Halbern and I become the preferred targets.

I get hit a few times, but manage to steady myself against the impacts and keep moving. The worst of the damage is a graze to the leg. My trousers immediately darken with blood, but I can still move normally. The blasts which strike my torso leave bruises as they slam into my vest, and one knocks the wind from me for a moment. Still, I'm mostly whole as we make it to the cover of our units and I'm glad I listened to my instinct to put the armor on.

Even though we're protected by the Blackbird I keep dragging Halbern until we're secure behind my Hallowstone's imposing silhouette. I lean the young man up against the carry, then put my cheek up against his face; can't tell if he's breathing or not.

Blood mixes with rain on his chest. His sigil is shattered. Silver covered in crimson.

The griffon screeches at me from its cage. It wants to fight. I force it down and activate my link.

"Dispatch. 072707. Officer down. Requesting chirurgeon's wagon and all available units. We're taking blasts from six unknown assailants with mixed arms."

I grab the downed officer's wand from his hip and return fire with it over the top of my unit. Seconds pass. "072707. Dispatch. Be advised that's a negative on the wagon. You're in an exclusion zone. Closest acceptable distance from the Warrens is three blocks northeast."

"Say again dispatch?" I reload.

"Pull back to the rendezvous point, Detective. Wagon incoming. Additional patrol units and watchtower detectives incoming."

"Eta?" I ask as I discharge more blasts. One of our assailants is forced down behind a planter.

"Five to ten minutes."

"Oh bugger me," I say. Not into the link. I'm too busy laying down blasts for that.

The spirit inside is clawing to get out and into the fray. After what happened in Heartcore I've kept it locked down tight. I'm still not sure I can trust it.

My Hallowstone catches fire as blasts from the fire rod take their toll. Stance is pinned behind the lorry. She's barely able to return fire with her weapon, and her cover is being degraded as the lorry's cheap bay is ablated by concentrated fire.

Do you want to fight? I ask my totem.

Hunt! Fight!

New rules, you bastard. I'm in control of me. You get to help.

I feel the beast rail at the thought, but it quiets. I sense a grudging acceptance, and an odd satisfaction.

Foreboding mixes with outright dread as I consider what that might mean.

I scramble back to the rear of my burning unit and manage to get the trunk open. I reach in and grab the rod, then fish around for the stack of extra crystals. Tucking them into my pocket, I check the disposition of our attackers. Good for us, they're not pressing forward.

The earth rod's strap slips comfortably around me as I secure the weapon across my back. With the Hallowstone rapidly warming from the flames I pull Halbern away and lay him out across the sidewalk a few feet away from the carry.

I grab the fallen officer's spare charges and tuck them into my duster. Almost as an afterthought I unsnap the pouch for his shackles and stuff them into a pocket. With six enemies to handle, I might need the extra restraints.

Then I turn around and seek contact with the Corporal. "Stance!" I shout.

"Yeah. I'm here." She looks terrified, but she keeps her voice level.

"You need to get your partner three blocks northeast. A wagon is on the way."

"I'm pinned. You go. Get Ste—Halbern to the wagon. I'll hold them off." She doesn't stumble over a single word outside of her partner's given name as she says it. Yet either the heat coming off my carry is distorting her face, or her eyes have filled with tears.

I glance at the spent crystals lying scattered on the ground next to the uniform. Even in a ward like Black Spit there's no way she's carrying much more charge. She's already chewed through more than I scavenged off her partner.

"Stance, I think you'd better let me."

"Detective, I—"

She's cut off by a volley from our attackers. I hear her scream and see the blood flowing from her hand as she jerks it to her chest. Her wand falls to the ground.

"That's an order, Corporal," I shout over the noise. "You wait until I give you cover. Get your partner, go through the alley down the street behind me, and get your arse down those blocks as fast as you can."

"Detective, we're pinned," she says through clenched teeth, as naked fear dances across her face.

But our attackers are amateurs. They reload nearly all at once, providing me with just enough of a lull.

"Not for long," I say as I shift Halbern's weapon and drop my own service wand out of its wrist sheath. I raise both wands and slide towards the front of my carry.

Then I let the griffon loose.

CHAPTER 3

The beast's consciousness slams into me, but I don't black out. The feeling is unlike any I've experienced. My companion spirit has always done my bidding in the world it occupies, or taken control in my reality. Only once have I ever been aware while it was in control, and that was during thoroughly unpleasant circumstances.

This time I'm the master of my body, and the totem is riding just behind my eyes.

We need to take them fast, I say to it. *You once told me we could fly, but all we need now is to run. Fast.*

I break cover in a crouch and raise both wands. My first pair of blasts take out an attacker armed with an earth rod. The figure goes down gurgling as the elementally hardened projectile tears through their throat.

The assailant next to my target is showered in arterial spray and drops to the ground. I rise up to sprint diagonally across the road.

Raw power flows through me.

I reach the opposite side of the road within a second, and duck into cover. The blasts of my enemies land far behind me.

My mind rejects what I've just done. I turn and check the distance from my burning vehicle. Impossible. It's close to fifty feet away from my current position.

I'm not the only one having a hard time reconciling what just happened with the realm of the possible. Voices pile atop each other in a jumbled mess.

"Shit! Where'd he go?"

"What the fuck?"

"He's gone!"

"Fuck, fuck. Rigger's dead!"

"Where's that damn cop?"

"Look at all the fucking blood, man!"

I tuck the officer's wand into the long custom pocket sewn inside my duster then slip mine back into its wrist sheath. Unlimbering the earth rod, I crank it to wide dispersion. I'm not sure how the spirit's power works, but I'm pretty sure I don't need it for what I'm about to do.

I reach up to my chest and jam my sigil's activation stud. My smoky black griffon flares to life, hovering atop the city's crest which sparkles gold. The symbol of my authority blazes on my chest as I step out from cover and start firing.

Screams assault my ears as the attackers are struck by the shards of rock summoned into being before the rod and propelled at high velocity in a wide cone. I hear the clatter of the pebbles as they strike everything in front of me.

At twenty feet away from the nearest of them the effect is less than fatal. But it's immensely painful and demoralizing. "NDPD!" I shout as I activate the rod again. "Drop your weapons." I fire another blast.

I'm greeted with mixed results. The two in front—who've taken the brunt of the rod's blasts—turn and run down the arcade. Two of the others drop their weapons. But the last fires his weapon.

Unfortunately for me, he's got a lightning pistol. Worse: he gets lucky.

The blast locks my muscles up and I list to the side. The rod falls free as I start to spasm. I'm stunned and falling.

Then the griffon catches me.

The spirit disperses the bolter's charge and thrusts my arm out to break my fall. I'm left panting on the ground as it recedes. My assailant pulls a long knife and steps over me.

I flop onto my back.

"Die, cop," he says and leans down to cut my throat.

I extend my arm and trigger the spring release, then activate my wand until the charge is out. Blood fountains from the man as the ice riddles his torso with holes. His corpse falls on me.

"Motherfucker!" shouts one of the others. Blasts from an ice wand strike the sidewalk next to me. I shove the corpse towards the renewed attack and roll away.

"Come on, let's go," says the only female voice. I scramble behind a carry and dig for a fresh crystal. I slam it home and peek around the corner.

One dead body. Nobody else visible.

I scoot back to the street side and check for anyone flanking. I'm clear.

My Hallowstone is ablaze. Just in front of it the blue and white is riddled with marks from the blasts it shielded Halbern and me from as I sought better cover for us. Another couple of sacrifices to Akala on Dead's Night.

I can't see Stance or Halbern. The earth rod the fallen officer dropped is also gone. I assume the Corporal grabbed the weapon as she went for Halbern. With any luck she's halfway down the alley already. I start to make a move to cross the empty street when my totemic beast beats at me.

Hunt!

I pull up short. *You want to go after them?* I ask my spirit.

Prey.

I know that I can walk away. I know that I *should* walk away. But months behind a desk have left me with a hunger for the chase.

Our masked assailants critically injured—if not killed—an NDPD officer and wounded two others. They destroyed my carry, and marred the patrol unit. They damaged other property—public as well as private—and risked civilian casualties by discharging their weapons without regard for where their blasts might land.

What are we waiting for, then? I ask the spirit.

It screeches in pleasure as I step out of cover, retrieve the rod, and head towards the Warrens.

With as far behind as I am—or, I suppose, *we are*—a little bit of speed seems in order. I check around the corner to ensure that nobody is waiting to waylay us. I see nothing but a long plaza lined on both sides with dilapidated storefronts.

I let the griffon know it's time to catch up to our quarry.

My first experience with the celerity of the spirit was so sudden and unexpected that I couldn't comprehend it. So during the second, I pay attention.

The haste with which we cover the ground in front of the shops as we surge towards the Warrens is preternatural.

When I was a lad—just a wee litlin of three or four—my father took me to see the griffons putting on aerial displays during mating season. I was fascinated with them. Maybe that's why the spirit chose me. Then again, maybe not.

But I was completely enthralled. The memory of that slow, arcing dance has stayed with me ever since. The majesty and serenity of the ritual made an impression.

Drawing on my bond with the totemic spirit of one of those regal beasts isn't particularly peaceful. It feels a lot more like I'd imagine a projectile fired out of a sniper's stave does. Fortunately there's no splat at the end.

But we do traverse an entire block within a handful of seconds. I pause to marvel at the feeling—and to be cautious crossing the street—but the next row of stores vanishes as the beast tosses out another burst of speed.

I'm standing across from the Warrens as I watch the last

of the attackers hustle down a tight alley which leads into the maze of the slum.

What else can I do? I give pursuit.

CHAPTER 4

Bugger me. That's my first thought as I duck inside. There's no way to use the kind of speed the griffon is capable of inside the Warrens. My initial impressions are first, that the descriptions I've heard don't do this section of Black Spit justice; and second, that I understand why the NDPD has a hands off policy.

I stow the wands and unlimber the earth rod as I scan the area. My heart is hammering. I'm not claustrophobic, but the tight walls of the alley and the looming balconies that press down from above give me pause.

I consider leaving again, but I'm close to the tail end of the attackers, so I press on instead. I flip the switch on the link, cutting its power. Doing so keeps dispatch from tracking me, and no doubt ordering me to withdraw. It also ensures that I'm not distracted by any incoming communications. Stuck with my own pace I find plenty of time to take in the sights, sounds, and smells of the Warrens.

The odors are those of refuse and waste, mixed with food, as well as the general press of the masses which inhabit the ghetto. I hear men and women; children and animals. The echoes of a micro-civilization going about its routine. I wonder if the noise is typical, or if the hive of activity is in high spirits because of Dead's Night.

The air is stale as I snake my way into the neighborhood. I find myself strangely dry. Many of the alleyways I walk through seem to be open to the sky, but the many stories of balconies above me keep the downpour largely at bay.

Prey! alerts the griffon.

I feel—no, smell—an orc just around the corner which lies before me. I'm struck by how keen the spirit's senses are as it shares the scent. The woman seems to have stopped to rest after her retreat. Even with my normal hearing I can hear her shuddering breaths as she tries to suck in enough air. I sidle up to the bend and have a peek. She's removed her mask and squatted down to catch her breath. Blood from the first tough I took down covers her clothes.

As she glances up, the earth rod is the first thing she sees. Her eyes lock onto it, and she presses back into the wall. She breaks her gaze away from my weapon only to have them drawn to my blazing sigil. Finally she settles on my eyes.

"NDPD," I say in a quiet voice. I don't really want to advertise, though by now plenty of people must know I'm here. All that's saving me from serious trouble is that clarions are notably scarce inside Black Spit, and almost unheard of in the Warrens. The city can't pay workers enough to install them in here.

She nods, so I let her know the score. "You're under arrest." Her pale green skin is slick with rain, but the griffon can smell her sweat. She's afraid. She knows I've killed two of her companions, and that I'm justified in using lethal force against a cop killer.

"Now," I say as I step closer. I tap my free finger against my sigil. "I'm going to tell them you cooperated with me. *If* you take me to round up your friends. The gold sigil means they trust me, savvy?"

Her throat works as she tries to speak. A croak comes out. She tries again a moment later and manages it. "Yes."

"Where's your weapon?" She shakes her head. "Where is it?"

"I don't have one."

"At the first sign of any trouble, you're probably going to die." I wiggle the rod. "Maximum spread. At this range you'll be lucky if you're not in two pieces." She rubs the minor wounds the rod inflicted earlier and licks her lips as she shudders.

I hand her my shackles and she puts them on behind her back. I search her. No weapons. No anything, actually. If she weren't covered in blood I wouldn't have been able to place her at the scene of the ambush.

"This way," the girl says as I finish my frisk, then she starts walking.

I follow, rod trained on the middle of her back.

We weave our way into the maze of buildings. I see lights dim as we approach, I hear hushed whispers as we pass. Gone are the nearby party noises. The whole slum is going to know I'm here soon. But I've got no other good options ahead of me, so I keep following the orc.

"Jaro lives in this building," my captive says as we stop at a darkened archway five minutes later. "I dunno if he's home, but this is his place."

"Jaro. He was with you?"

"Yes."

"You're going in front." She starts to move for the door, but I stop her with a hand on her shoulder. "Anything funny happens, you get to die first." She tenses, but I see her head bob.

We head into the tenement building and wind our way up rickety flights of stairs. Four stories up she moves off the landing and into a tight hallway. If the alleyways were narrow, this is crushing. I have to duck to pass under the glow of the lights. I'm fairly sure if it comes to a shootout I'm not going to be able to miss whatever is in front of me.

Of course the discomforting thought which logically follows that realization is that I doubt they'll miss me either. My hands start to sweat a little. I wipe them on my trousers.

The girl stops, then points her chin at a door to her right. I stand her in front of the portal, then knock. A poke from the tip of the rod so she gets the idea follows. I slip Halbern's wand out from my duster and grip it in my left hand.

"Hey Kina," says a young man's voice as the door opens. "You look worse than I f—"

The wand directed at his head cuts the young man's words

off. He blinks. I jerk my head and he nods slowly then backs up, staring at the tip of the weapon. The three of us move slowly into his apartment.

The combination of scant furnishing outside of a large couch and larger tapestry, and the general disarray of the studio, spells out a young bachelor's residence. "That bathroom empty, Jaro?" I ask.

"Yeah. Are you fucking out of your mind?"

For a second I think he's asking the girl. Then I realize he's wondering why I'm coming after them in the Warrens. "Maybe. But if you think about it, lad, that just means you need to be afraid of me. Kina—is that your name, lass?" She nods. "Kina here has just been subjected to an earth rod in her kidneys for the past ten minutes or so. How'd that feel?"

"Shitty," she says, "thanks for asking."

"Don't mention it." I wiggle the wand slightly. "See kid, there's no procedures for going into a crime infested ghetto and rooting out a gang of wankers who thought it'd be a good idea to attack officers of the NDPD. I'm making this shit up as I go along, aye?"

"You're dead when he finds out," he says.

"Your boss, your leader, that's who you're talking about?"

"Shut up, Jaro," says the girl. I poke her with the rod she lets out a grunt as it digs into her back.

"Who, Jaro?"

"Fuck you, cop. Arrest me then." He smiles. It's unpleasant.

"She's wearing my shackles." I smile and level the wand at his chest. The look on his face tells me he finds it unpleasant.

"I'll tell yo—"

The girl leans towards him and half shouts. "Fucking shut up, Ja—" she yelps as I jab her in the back with the rod.

The sandy-haired young man continues. "Ammon Blackface..." His pause seems meant to be significant. I wait. "Ammon the Sorceror," he says, then shakes his head. "He was in the carriage. He sent for us, so we came."

"Sent for you how?" I ask.

"Magic. Raw magic. He has real power, cop." Jaro works up some more courage. "You're a dead man when he finds out, and by now he's probably on the way."

Magic with any kind of real power to it is rare. The thought of facing down someone with actual command of it is not a pleasant one, but I've got a mission. "He going to bring your friends with?"

"What?"

"The other two. I need to arrest them. And this Ammon. Your boss—or whatever he is—as well. Since he was in the carry, and gave the orders."

His eyes widen. "You're damned crazy."

"Mmm. I've been bored lately. Needed some exercise." I do feel like I've crossed a line, and I'm not sure when it was. I wonder if it was when I broke cover, after I'd downed the two and scattered the rest, or maybe just once I'd apprehended Kina.

Whatever the case, I'm stuck with only one way out. Moving forward.

I step back and fish for the keys to my restraints. I toss them to Jaro. "Undo her right hand, close the shackle around your left wrist, then give me the keys." He looks wary, but complies. Mostly. "Left to left, lad. That's your right. I want you facing opposite directions when you move. Makes it harder for you to run away."

He switches hands and throws the keys back "You don't want that temptation anyway," I say as I pocket the ring. "I'd have to shoot you."

"I'm not running," he says.

"You can start walking though." I point towards the door and step into the tiny kitchenette. "So, where do your friends hang out?" They file past me, Kina in the lead. "Go ahead and start walking in their direction."

"Why?" asks the girl as she steps out into the hallway.

"One of you is a cop killer," I say, hoping it's a lie. "It's my job to bring you in and find out which one it is."

"Be smarter to try and get out alive," she says under her breath.

I shake my head as I follow. "Now where's the fun in that?"

CHAPTER 5

The rain has trailed off by the time we get outside. At street level that means being nearly dry. Outside of the pools of filthy water and the occasional drops from rainwater collected by the network of balconies, at least.

I feel the griffon's longing as I look up. It wants to be higher, running and leaping across those close-set terraces. If it wouldn't attract even more attention I'd do it, but I have captives to consider, and announcing myself any more than I have might wake the interest of others, not just the criminals I'm hunting.

The Warrens has one of the lowest crime rates in the entire city-state. It's difficult for those outside to know what goes on inside the cramped slum, but I read a series of articles a few years back by a herald who claimed to have lived in the Warrens for a year doing research. He wrote about the discipline enforced by the various powers-that-be, and the genuine, neighborly nature of the inhabitants in general.

I'd doubted it at the time, and the piece had been controversial, to say the least. But nothing I've seen since entering the Warrens tonight has made me doubt the possibility that the man had been sharing the truth hidden beneath the surface of the ghetto. There have been no sounds of fighting. No wand blasts. No angry voices.

Not even before the silence presently reigning started to spread. A hush no doubt driven by news of my presence.

There's an interloper present, and the network doesn't need clarions to spread that news.

A few times since breaching the walls of this place I've had the overwhelming feeling of being watched. But try as I might, I haven't been able to spot any eyes. The griffon hasn't been much help either, though a few times I've felt like it was on the verge of spotting something I'd missed.

Jaro looks sullen as we shuffle down the pathways Kina selects. He looks back at me often. I keep the rod ready, though his eyes betray nothing more than resignation to his current circumstances.

Better to not give him the impression that I've gone soft though. So I flash him hard looks and gesture menacingly with the rod.

I'm too busy watching my charges to check my chrono—a fact which is beginning to bother me—but what seems like ten or fifteen minutes pass before we stop short at the outlet to our current sideway.

"Antolio and Ganzer live in that building, on the roof," says the girl. She points up at an unusually tall, and visible structure. We're standing at the entrance to a broad open area that might qualify as a yard. Beyond the space is the tower block. It's a rarity.

No balconies project from its face. The giant is set far apart from the buildings which surround it. I can clearly see the cloudy skies for the first time since entering the Warrens.

"They have a good view," I say. I glance at the windows along the face. A quick count gives me sixteen stories. I knew about the half dozen of these monstrosities crammed into the neighborhood from reading the articles, though I don't recall a reason for their existence ever being given.

Its presence here makes little sense as I stare up at it. But like it or not, this is where the final two attackers are. I've got a duty to bring them in.

"If they're home, they'll know that you're here." She pauses and tilts her head. "Well, that we're all here."

"Shouldn't keep them waiting then, should we?" Kina shrugs, Jaro looks at the ground, and I point the wand at the entrance. "Let's go say hello."

It takes me about two seconds to realize how ugly things may get when we get inside.

The tunnel leading into the building is deep and wide, but not very high. Outside of any balconies which might be present on other sides of the structure, it may be the only way out. Given how old the block is, there may not even be fire escapes.

It's like walking into a cop trap baited with tasty criminals.

Not only is the structure taller than most in the Warrens—or the rest of Black Spit for that matter—but it's a lot more open. That might have been a nice thing at one time. A century in the past these may have been marvelous dwellings.

But the reality of the current situation is that what luxurious space which used to exist within the confines of the central forum is now completely taken up by a makeshift settlement. The entrance gives way to small buildings of varying materials and design, packed and stacked within the grounds. There are tight pathways leading between the hovels, and a network of interconnecting walkways which span the gaps between the floors of the shacks. Some are as many as five floors, though the tallest barely come up to the bottom of the fourth story of the actual tenement.

Yet the most astounding part is that this base is just the start of the hidden core. Strung across the entirety of the close is a network of hanging platforms which reaches up towards the sky. There are so many layers of haphazardly placed structures that I can barely make out a few bits of the night above. Drops of water—from the rain, which is starting to pick up again—filter down from above, rolling off the latticework of bridges and scaffolds which make up the suspended hamlet.

Unlike outside—where the tightness of the alleyways limits visibility, and allows residents to avoid intruders with ease—I can see many people going about their business. Music resonates throughout the area. Somewhere in the center there's a large gathering with many people laughing and talking. A Dead's Night celebration at the heart of this behemoth from another time.

"What's the matter, cop?" asks Jaro. I glance down at him and realize my mouth is ever so slightly open.

I shake my head. "It's—"

"Dirty? Pathetic?"

"I was going to say ingenious, actually. Marvelous resourcefulness." I shrug. "Completely illegal, of course. But I'm a homicide detective. I catch murderers, not people violating building codes." I grin at him. "Bad luck for you. If you'd shot up a housing inspector you wouldn't be in shackles."

"We should go," says Kina as she pulls on Jaro's arm. "I don't really want to catch a stray blast if anyone decides you're not welcome."

I consider her thought as I follow. "That likely?"

"No," she says as we slip past a couple of full rubbish bins. "But tonight isn't the night to tempt fate, is it?"

"No, it's not." We make our way to a stairwell in the corner of the courtyard. I see no sign of a lift, and Kina doesn't pause before mounting the steps and heading up towards our destination. I didn't actually expect to find anything other than stairs given the age of the structures in the Warrens, but sixteen flights followed by a showdown isn't an appealing thought.

As we climb I find myself drawn to the view each time the core is revealed. Every new level brings with it a shift in perspective. A reveal of some new detail.

Though the structures were impressive enough when I was looking up from the bottom, the true intricacy of the design is revealed as we ascend. I find myself caught by the clever use of materials which have obviously been scavenged from rubbish bins and scrap yards. I doubt even a quarter of the materials were new when they were put in place. Ready supplies of repurposed parts lie neatly stacked along the walkways which offer access to the apartments within the building itself.

I'm nearly beyond caring if anyone knows we're coming by the time we reach the seventh floor. We're completely exposed as we climb. I come to accept that I have no element of surprise.

Outside of the power which lurks within me, at least.

We come out on the top, on the sixteenth floor, and Kina pauses. She points down the gallery towards a door. "That's the only access to the roof."

"And they know we're here." I say.

She nods. I consider my options. If I leave the two of them behind—even secured to whatever is handy—the chances of them being around when I get back are minimal. Taking them with just gives me more enemies in one place. Worse, I'd be risking their safety.

No good options means finding the best bad one.

"Scared, cop?" asks Jaro.

"No, just trying to decide what to do with you. I figure there's a good chance whoever walks out onto that rooftop is going to get a blast to the face. Kina's been helpful in getting us here. That means you're going out first."

He pales. Kina looks grateful and moves back towards me. The young man starts to plead with me. "Come on, I was just—"

"You were just walking," I say, cutting him off. I suspect it's the rod I've raised to head level that convinces him, but he does turn and start moving towards the door. He takes his time, but I can't blame him.

It gives me time to take a last look over the edge as we move. The entirety of the settlement spirals away below me. I consider the article from years back and admit to myself that it's possible the Warrens isn't actually a hive of criminal activity.

At least not the kind that preys on its own.

"Do you like it?" asks Kina. Her voice is quiet. I get the feeling she doesn't want Jaro involved in the conversation.

"I think it's wondrous," I say, keeping my voice low in turn.

"I was born in a hanging garden." She gets a far off look in her eyes for a moment, then continues. "Not this one though. One of the others."

I consider that what works in one is probably applied to the others, so Kina's childhood home would have been similar to this. I wonder for a moment how many people live in the Warrens. It must be a huge number; the buildings are densely packed, and the apartments seem tiny. The rest of the city-state ignores the neighborhood, so I've never seen a proper census, but it must be incredibly populous.

"That's a lovely name for them," I say. "Do people really grow things here?"

She nods. "This is the wrong season for most plants, so you can't see much." She points to a few open areas which look like sandboxes. "But most of the rest of the year, yes."

"Amazing."

Kina jerks her chin towards the space beyond the railing. "The top three or four levels are for the best farmers. They get the most light." She frowns. "Usually the roof as well. But not here."

I open my mouth to ask about the roof but Jaro jerks open the door and pulls her inside. I adjust the spread of the earth rod, check the charge on Halbern's wand, take three deep breaths, and slip through the door after them.

Kina's eyes widen as I walk through the portal. Her mouth opens.

The griffon screeches.

My head explodes in a field of stars, and I go black.

CHAPTER 6

It turns out I'm not dead.

Either that or dead is much more painful than I expected it to be.

My pulse hammers in my skull. It's difficult to breathe. I have a splitting headache.

I'm inverted. Something is wrapped around my ankles, and I'm hanging. My duster streams out below me. I'm hanging over the hanging gardens.

I laugh.

I wince.

The griffon is pissed. I struggle with it for a moment before getting it calmed. I'm surprised—if relieved—that it hasn't taken over.

I need power, I say to the totem. *Go gather some.* I feel the spirit flee and spiral away towards the ground. It gives me vertigo and I close my eyes again.

"You awake, cop?" Jaro. He's somewhere nearby. I ignore him.

"Yeah, he's awake," says another male voice. A deep one. The resonance is impressive, and I immediately imagine a huge man behind me.

"Can we drop him yet?"

"Not yet."

I open my eyes and look for them, but I'm facing the wrong way. From the angle I figure I'm on the roof. I look for landmarks to orient myself with, but the bridges and platforms all look strange and unfamiliar. I manage to glance a bit off to the side and catch a glimpse of rooftop before Jaro intrudes on my thoughts again.

"I want to hear him scream as he falls."

"No, Jaro, we're waiting," says another man's voice. This one is a clear, melodic tenor.

"You still there, Kina?" I ask.

"Ha, he is awake!" shouts Jaro. "Drop him! Drop him! Dro—" His voice is cut off by a choking sound.

"Enough," says the bass voice.

"Kina?" I ask. I twist a little bit. Rope creaks above me.

"I'm here, cop." There's a note in her voice I can't explain, but I know that I'm not alone. Better, I can feel the noose around my feet. I'm not chained.

"Good. So, do I have the pleasure of addressing the gentlemen I was looking for?"

"Yeah, they're here." She doesn't sound too happy about it.

"Antolio?" I wiggle around to get a better look at my duster as it hangs off of me. It looks like someone emptied the pockets. Or they emptied themselves when I was hauled upside down.

"Yes, detective," says the tenor. "I'm Antolio, and this is my garden. Like it?"

"I love it, actually. Ask Kina."

The orc chimes in. "Yes, that's true, he said—"

"Drop him," says Jaro in a half croak.

"Ask again and see what happens," says the man with the rumbling voice.

"Ganzer?" I ask. I rock myself slightly. I can feel the pressure of the folding blade inside my boot. Whoever searched me missed it.

"Yeah," he says. "Don't take this to mean I like you. You killed Rigger. I just think Jaro is a fucking idiot."

"Seems an apt description."

"Dro—" Jaro starts up, but stops as if he's choked off his own words.

Antolio picks up in the wake of the young man's burst of

self-control. "So while we're waiting, for my own amusement, why did you come here?"

"You two were named as being part of the ambush that killed an NDPD officer. I've come to take you in."

Ganzer laughs. It's deep and cruel. "You've come to take us in?" he asks. "How?"

"More importantly," says Antolio. "Why were we named, Kina?"

"I wouldn't go too hard on her," I say. "She had an earth rod staring her in the face."

"I'll admit that we were surprised to hear that a cop was in the Warrens at all."

"The four of you were involved in the murder of a patrol officer. Did you think that would go unanswered?"

"Honestly? Yes."

I keep stalling. "What we can do here is try and get to the bottom of the events." My hands are free, but I don't think I can shake the knife free into them. Not without risking dropping it. "Then, once I have the truth, I'll decide what charges I'm going to take each of you in on."

"What?" asks Ganzer.

"It's obvious, isn't it?" I know I can levitate the knife if it's in my hand, but I've never tried pulling it out of my boot. Besides, the griffon isn't with me right now. "I need to know who was carrying what weapons."

"You need to hang there until Ammon gets here," Antolio says.

"Ammon. He's the one Jaro called a sorcerer. But he boosts carriages?"

"He has power," says Jaro. He's getting agitated.

"Yeah, scary, he called for backup. So did the officers you attacked. All things considered, on the backup front I'd say Ammon loses. After all, two of your friends are dead."

"You're hanging off of a roof," say Antolio.

"Aye. But look, only one of you is guilty of murder." Divide and conquer. "The others are just accessories, and cutting a deal means less time inside."

"None of us is going down for anything."

"See, that's what all of you think. But the fact is that one you killed a cop. All of you assaulted two other officers. You're all responsible for the destruction of government property. There's a reckoning to pay."

"All right, I'm with Jaro," says Ganzer. "Let's just drop him."

"I had a fire rod," says Kina.

"There we go," I say. "Now, can I get the truth from the rest of you?"

"Fuck you, cop," says Ganzer.

"I know what kind of weapon killed officer Halbern." Lies and more lies. All I know is that one of the four probably discharged the blast that downed the officer. But it's awfully hard to see anything to lose in lying when you're hanging from the roof of a sixteen story building. "All I need to know is which one of you was using it."

"Nobody is talking," says Antolio.

"See, there's where you're wrong. Kina just did. She knows she can save herself months—maybe even bloody *years*—in prison, just by cooperating. I bet it was Jaro though."

Jaro can't resist the bait. "No way! I had an earth rod on full spread."

"Shut up," says Ganzer.

"I couldn't have hit him that bad! I was just trying to scare you off Ammon, that's it."

"You fucking idiot." Flesh strikes flesh and someone expels air hard. I assume Ganzer has just crammed his fist into Jaro's gut. Things aren't likely to get much better for me.

"See, I've accounted for four of the weapons now. This is going well. Why don't you tell me, Antolio, was it you, or the muscle? Which one of you killed the officer?"

"You know, I think Jaro might be right after all," says the tenor. I hear movement close behind me.

I reach out to the spirit and brush it through our bond. It's far away and full of power gathered from the tide.

Give me everything you've got, I say to it.

Antolio is close behind me. I can hear him stop, then shuffle a bit.

Then my totem returns.

To me it sounds like the roar of waves on the shore. Like the walls of the Warrens have crumbled and revealed the ocean. The surge of power which the griffon is driving before it is massive. I can feel—even see—the flood as it rises up from below.

I scream as it hits me.

CHAPTER 7

I'm drowning in power.

I twist and spin as it engulfs me. I can't tell which way is up. I'm blinded by the radiance of the energy. Nothing but the thunder of its presence fills my ears.

My gut surges for a moment as I feel weightless.

Fly! demands the griffon.

I feel acceleration and force myself to see through the haze of raw magic. The ground is coming.

Fly!

So I do.

Like a fledgling out of the nest, Detective Griffon falls from the sky and flaps his wings. The results are crude, but somewhat amazing given that humans—as a rule—cannot fly.

I change course in the middle of my free fall and slam into a rope bridge several stories below the roof.

Swearing and shouting echoes from above as I bounce. Like a chick tumbling from a cliff, I resume my rapid descent.

A suspension cable is the next obstacle in my path. I veer wildly towards it, nearly overshooting. I get my arms tangled around it and jerk to a halt. My head protests. My arms protest. My stomach gives up, and I vomit.

I nearly shake myself free as I convulse, but somehow I manage to hang on. As the heaving stops I work my feet free of the noose which they'd suspended me from and swing myself up to the thick rope. Panting, I hang from all four limbs for a moment.

Then the blasts start to rain down.

I'm hit by some of the spread of an earth rod. My left leg jerks from the pain—it's the second time I've been shot in it tonight—and my lower extremities swing free. Ice rains down past me. A shard hits me in the side of my chest, impacting on the vest but skittering away from the angle. I have to tense up to keep from losing my tenuous grasp on the rope.

I start to swing hand over hand as fast as I can. The spirit speeds me along and I cover the twenty foot gap to the nearest platform in a few seconds. As I reach it, I flip myself up onto what appears to be someone's balcony. The wooden roof above me is hammered with blasts and starts to splinter as I scramble around to the lee side of the hovel. Female screams sound from inside.

"NDPD!" I shout. "Get down."

Blinking hard, I try to focus on the real, physical world. The power flowing around me becomes slightly less opaque and I start to orient myself. My boot still contains the knife, so I pull it out and flick it open. I want to turn my link on and report officer in distress, but whoever searched me only missed the blade.

The blasts stop and I hear shouting from above. I'm too far away and my head is too full of power to make out what they're saying, but from the booming I can tell Ganzer is enraged.

A few feet away is a door. I can hear weeping from within, punctuated by choked whispers. I crawl over to it and knock. "NDPD," I say again, this time softly. "Are you injured?"

The door opens and a tiny child peeks out. It takes me a moment to realize it's actually a teenage gnome. She's crying. "My mom is hurt," she sobs. "Please...help..."

I crawl inside and she shuts the door behind me. An older gnome is lying unconscious on the floor of the two-room dwelling. She's bleeding from a large hole in her slender leg.

"Is there a chirurgeon nearby?" I ask as I cast my eyes about the area. I spot a scarf and grab it.

The girl sobs "N—no."

"Is there a clarion?"

She shakes her head. "Only up top."

"Shit. Ok, my name is Griffon." Normally I'd repeat that I'm a police officer, but here in the Warrens I'm not sure how reassuring it would be.

"I'm Keesee."

"Keesee. Good. I'm going to get your mother help." I tie the leg off with the scarf then tighten it with a long shard which has broken off from roof. The flow of blood starts to slow as I wind it tighter. It looks like she's lost a lot, but blood is tricky. She's terribly pale, but I don't know her normal tone. The girl has light skin, even with her cheeks flushed with fear. "Keesee, I have to leave you with her while I call for help."

"Don't police have devices to talk to each other?"

"The men who hurt your mother took my link."

She nods. "What do I do?"

"Just make sure that you keep this tight on her leg. If you let go she can bleed more."

"Ok." She sniffles and takes the tourniquet from me. "Hurry."

I crawl back to the door. My eyes are adjusting to the glow but a niggling thought bothers me. "Keesee, am I glowing?"

"What?"

"Do I give off light?"

"No? Why would you glow?"

"They hit me on the head. Everything seems a little funny because of it, that's all." I give her a smile and push the door open. "Don't worry. I'll get help. You just keep that pressure on her leg."

I take a deep breath, tighten my grip on the knife, and slip out of the dwelling.

CHAPTER 8

"He landed right over there," says Jaro as he steps around the corner. I'm tucked into an alcove behind a pair of overflowing rubbish bins. Fortunately I already lost my lunch. The smell is abysmal. I watch as the young man walks out onto the bridge and heads towards Keesee's home. My stomach tightens as I see that he's armed with an earth rod. My time is running out.

"I still don't know how the fuck he didn't just fall *down*," says Antolio. "I dropped him straight. He was barely moving, just howling. But they all do that. Nobody has ever gone anywhere but the bone pile. Not even that elf who thrashed so much I thought he was going to work himself loose."

He crosses in front of my position with an ice wand. A big one. The kind that might get lucky and penetrate a patrol officer's vest. The slim man steps out onto the bridge and lifts the weapon towards the damaged dwelling.

"Looked like a doll being thrown around," says Ganzer. "My sister's kid swings her doll around like that." The brute crosses in front of me. Only he's not a brute. He's a scrawny dwarf. He's carrying a fire rod though, so he's still a credible threat.

I'm out of time. Jaro is almost to the door. The gnomes are in danger.

I slip out from behind the bins and head towards Ganzer, knife clenched inverted in my fist, ready for close work. I spot Kina as I break cover. She's five yards away, holding a service issue ice wand. Turning, I crouch lower and get ready to rush her. She lowers the wand and puts it on the ground. I jerk my head and she backs away.

"You in there, cop?" asks Jaro from in front of the gnomes' home.

Protocol demands I announce my presence and demand surrender. Protocol can get buggered when I've got a knife and three armed enemies.

I take Ganzer low, in the back of the knee. The blade slices cleanly through clothing and flesh. He screams and crumples. I elbow him in the back of the head and he falls. His rod skitters away and tumbles off the bridge.

Antolio raises his wand and discharges it. Ice slams into the bridge next to me as I throw myself into the rope railing. It bends perilously and threatens to spill me over the edge. Behind me a wand coughs and the slender man screams as he's hit in the shoulder.

He's raising his wand to respond to Kina's betrayal when I slam into him, taking him down. The impact of my tackle is joined by a hit to the back from an ice blast from Kina. The vest takes it but I lose my knife in the bargain. For a moment I wonder if she's trying to hit me, then I'm too busy grappling with Antolio.

I've got the advantage in mass, but he's clearly a fighter and my reach doesn't mean much on the ground. If anything, I realize my mistake was in believing Ganzer was the muscle of the group. Even injured, Antolio manages to get blows in to my face with his elbows as we land.

I bear down on top of him with all my weight and he locks his legs around mine to mitigate my advantage. He catches me with a head butt as I struggle to free my legs and I feel blood start to flow down my face.

"Fuck you, cop!" screams Jaro. I hear running footsteps. If he gets close enough I'm dead. The fact that Antolio might catch stray pellets is little comfort.

Behind me the service wand barks again. I hear a gurgle followed by a thud, and the bridge trembles.

Antolio tries to bring his own wand to bear. I slam his hand into the slats beneath us three times before he releases it. The weapon bounces up the bridge deck, but doesn't fall. He catches me with a cross and I feel the world spin.

I bring my arm up in time to block the next blow to my face, but a quick hit the the ribs follows, and three more chase that one.

"Move," says Kina. She's right behind me.

"No," I say. I'm not sure she can hear me though, given all the grunting I'm doing as I take blows from the slender man. "Don't." I block a poorly thrown punch and get a couple of good hits in on him. He spits blood and teeth as he lunges up with a jab to my throat.

I'm out of air as I catch the offending arm and wrench it upward. He gives a half scream. Then I break it.

That's worth a full scream.

I flip him onto his face and twist his arms—one shot, one broken—behind his back, then I shift my weight and kneel on him. Hard. After a few seconds of that he simply passes out in agony, or maybe from loss of blood. The shot to his shoulder is leaking.

I leave him face down on the bridge and recover his wand, careful to pick it up with the tail of my duster and slip it inside the long inner pocket. My knife is lying just beyond it. I pick the blade up, wipe it off on Antolio, and fold I back up.

"What now?" asks Kina.

I look over at Jaro as I tuck the knife into my duster. The orc shot him through the throat as he charged me. His eyes are wide and he's almost bled out. No chance to save him.

Ganzer is still crying in agony back at the beginning of the span. He's swearing at me in dwarven. The epithets are unflattering; almost enough to make me blush.

I turn around. Kina has the wand leveled at my chest. I tap my duster with my palm. "Was Antolio carrying this wand the whole night?"

She nods.

I sigh. I'm tired. I'm hurt. But I don't feel like testing my luck and trying for a miracle cure in Heartcore, even if I do have a lot of power left. I steady myself and continue. "I can't be sure if it's the weapon used on the officer, you know that, right?"

"It was," she says. "Antolio was there, and he was the only one using an ice wand. *That* ice wand."

"You'll testify?"

She shakes her head. "I'm going to disappear."

"You can have protective custody."

"No." The wand remains pointed at me. I recognize it as Halbern's.

"Fine. Where's my link, Kina?"

"Ganzer had it." I nod and start walking towards him. "Stop!"

"I need my link. Ganzer had it. Either you get it or I do."

"Hold on." She steps back carefully and bends down to rifle through the fallen dwarf's pockets. He's barely conscious now. I figure I hit the artery. Less deadly than higher on the leg, but he's in danger too.

"Want to tie his jacket off around his leg when you're done?"

"No." She throws me the link.

"No?" I trigger the device and watch it surge to life.

"I'm a poor girl from the Warrens and I don't have a lot of skills that look good on a resume."

I consider the information and nod. "Hard to get out."

"I was going to join the Army, but before I signed my mother got sick. I'm all she has." She shakes her head. "I'm not proud of it, but I've worked for Ammon for six months now. Done all kinds of odd jobs at his behest, you know? It pays well and with her sick...well, she's probably even dying. The potions and powders the alchemists have for her, even though I know they won't save her...they're all expensive."

"You were really going to join the Army?"

"I was dropfighter training approved."

I widen my eyes and pull my head back. Dropfighters are just a step shy of Special Operations Directorate. They aren't even close to run of the mill infantry. Their insertion into combat zones is accomplished via the same kind of specialized high altitude airships SOD uses for covert missions. The only way to get approval for training before enlisting is exceptional physical aptitude.

"I was a lieutenant in the SOD."

"That dream is gone now."

"Maybe. Trust me though, new dreams have a way of showing up."

"Like being a cop?"

"Like that."

"Anyway, it means I've seen what Ganzer has done to people. So fuck you, cop. He can bleed out." She smiles as she says it. There's no malice in her tone. Not for me at least.

"He'll go down for a long while, Kina." I shrug. "He'll get out, sure, but not any time soon."

"Dwarves live too long. Even his twisted, sickly ass."

I nod. "Maybe. Good luck, and leave the wand when you go."

I turn away from her and make the call.

CHAPTER 9

I watch as the Airborne Tactical Unit airship lands and dumps a Rapid Response Unit team out. I can see the specialists securing the roof, and catch sight of a trauma team following in the armed officers' wake.

There are only a handful of airships in the ATU. Most of the unit's work is done by golems. The automatons take up less space, and aren't risking any lives. Well, no lives in the air anyway. But for this kind of job there's always a few vehicles on standby to be tasked with moving men and equipment across the city.

Still, it may be the first time in the department's history that an airship has landed on a roof in the Warrens.

The four chirurgeons make their way down a couple of minutes later. I lead them past my two prisoners, and Jaro's corpse, to Keesee's mother. I inform the team lead that she gets attention first.

I get some backtalk from the man about triage, so I let my wand slide free. Not that I raise it; just repeat myself.

The gnome gets treated first.

They take care of Ganzer at almost the same time though. After all, it doesn't take four to handle a single victim. The other half of the team is all over the dwarf as soon as they see that I've controlled Antolio's shoulder bleed.

My efforts to stabilize my prisoners took place after I cut the connection to dispatch. I'd turned around to find Kina gone, and Halbern's wand lying on the bridge. Ganzer was first on my list. He'd passed out at some point during my request for backup, and by the time I got to him he was even more sickly-looking than he'd been before.

Still, the NDA's Advanced Operator School wasn't all about how to kill in new and interesting ways. All SOD soldiers get significant medical training. I may have lacked the devices a trauma team comes with, but my basic first aid skills are top notch. I was able to slow the dwarf's bleeding enough to keep him alive.

Unfortunately for Kina, it looks like Ganzer will live. If she's lucky he wasn't conscious enough to remember what she said about him.

Of course her bigger problem is likely to come from her former employer. Ammon never showed up, so I didn't have the chance to test the theory that he's a charlatan. I feel odd even considering it, but the truth of the matter is that I'll probably never know if he truly is anything like me.

The NDPD stays out of the Warrens, and Ammon seems like the type to keep himself to the shadowy confines of this maze. Besides, if he's any kind of real Sorcerer I'm willing to bet he'll realize running into me is a bad plan. If the Great Mage Wars taught the talented anything, it's that facing off against others who have power is never a sure thing.

Antolio is the last one to get treatment. His care comes at the hands of the RRU team's medic. I doubt the Corporal's training is much better than mine, but with the splint pilfered from the chirurgeons' gear, he temporarily immobilizes the broken arm. My work on the shoulder seems to have slowed the blood loss to a trickle, but the uniform wraps the wound for good measure. On the face of it Halbern's shooter seems completely out of danger.

More's the pity.

As we go about the business of extracting the pair of criminals, the bystanders, and the corpse, the inhabitants of the hanging garden keep to themselves. I do spot a few eyes peeking out at us, but—unlike at every other scene I've worked—there are no outright gawkers lined up.

During the slow load of the casualties—which is hindered by how crowded the airship is going to be on the way out—I search the roof for my belongings. I manage to recover everything which was liberated from me when I was rendered senseless.

Including my lucky fedora, which I find hung up on the edge of the roof where it threatens to tumble down into the courtyard below.

Finally I climb into the airship and settle into a seat between Keesee and Sergeant Brewer, the RRU team leader. The three of us share the bench next to the injured gnome.

The crystal drive spins up and we lift off gently. As we gather speed Brewer nudges me. "Mind me asking what you thought you were doing, Detective?" The Sergeant's voice carries no malice, just a hint of curiosity.

I shrug because it's obvious. "Pursuing suspects who'd attacked officers of the NDPD."

"Into the Warrens?"

I nod. "Aye. And ta very much for the extraction, Sergeant. Walking out might not have gone over too well."

"You're welcome, but we didn't get a choice in the matter. Rumor has it that Corporal Stance got her Captain to start throwing his weight around central."

I raise an eyebrow. "Really?"

Brewer laughs. "Way I heard it, the Captain said you were the only one with the balls to go in since he'd been on the Job, and that we owed it to you to get your ass out again."

"Glad Stance had my back."

"She says you took on six suspects—wounded, alone, and only armed with standard service issue weapons—just to give her the chance to extract her partner."

My face warms. "I did. How's Halbern? The officer. Did he, ah..."

Brewer lets out a low whistle. "I heard that the chirurgeons almost lost him three times."

"But he'll live." The kid seemed nice. He didn't deserve to

die for doing his job.

None of us ever do.

Brewer nods. "You know, the way Stance tells the story, you're getting a commendation. And she didn't even know you were bringing out two suspects, or that you'd killed three others."

I shake my head. "Just two. The third was killed by a stray burst. Not mine."

"Justice and death, Detective," he says. Respect rings clear in his tone.

I nod. The NDPD's official motto is: *In one hand, justice; in the other, death.* My theory is that when the department was formed two hundred years ago the original sentiment of *if you fuck with us, we'll kill you* was deemed to lack poetry.

"Are they going to prison?" Keesee asks.

I turn towards her and smile. "It might be tough to get them long sentences, but yes, they *will* be going away. For a number of years at the very least."

"But why not for a long time?"

"Antolio will go down for attempted murder, and he'll get the maximum because he tried to kill a cop. That never sits well with the magistrates. Plus, he's the one who hit your mother, so he'll get assault with a deadly weapon, even though he didn't aim at her."

"But not murder."

"Nobody died." I think of Jaro and the other two attackers I'd left lying on the street. "Well, not anyone who wasn't breaking the law."

"Sure. Nobody died...this time." She says it quietly. Her face is haunted; eyes far away. I let her work it through. After fifteen seconds or so she shakes herself and looks at me again. "I've seen him hang people before. I've seen them fall."

"How many times?"

"Too many."

"Do you know who any of the victims were?"

She nods. "A few of them, yeah. One was just a kid. Jarien.

He was a year or two older than me. My friend Siyra had crush on him."

"Would you be willing—"

"Yes."

"You didn't let me finish."

She shakes her head, hard. "They almost killed my mother. I'm going to say what they've done to anyone who will listen."

"All right. We'll talk about that soon. First, just worry about being there for her." I wave at the injured gnome. Keesee sniffles and a tear rolls down her cheek.

Brewer leans in and pats me on the back. "Three offenders dead, two in custody, and a witness dead-set on testifying? That's what I call an amazing job, Detective." He tilts his head. "Where's your partner tonight?"

I turn to look over my shoulder and out the window. There are fires dotting the city. I can see heavy crowds in some of the open plazas. But up here there's no noise outside of the airship's crystal drive.

"Out there," I say, waving at my city. "My partner is out there."

MIDNIGHT SORROWS

EPILOGUE

It's funny how much you can welcome something as mundane as a late night call to go in to work when you're just recently retired. You don't realize how much you're going to miss the Job until you're sitting on your ass at two in the afternoon, staring at the tapestry wondering if you should buy that new powder that will keep your hair from going gray. Missing the Job was about all I did now.

Well, outside of drinking. But I'd been doing that a long, long time.

I was glaring at the ruins of a piece of wood—all because some smartass from Robbery Unit had suggested I take up carving—when the clarion chimed. I tossed the shredded piece of aspen, grabbed my bourbon, and took it with me as I grabbed the horn.

"Yeah," I said as I brought it to my ear. Nobody calls me who doesn't know me. Or if they do, fuck 'em.

"Good, Thief, I'm glad you're awake," said the familiar voice of my former-Captain. He's still Captain, of course. I'm just a former-Detective.

"I sleep when it's light out now, Trawler."

"You always loved graveshift."

He's not wrong about that. I hated primeshift. I can work on just a few hours of sleep though, when I have to. So for years at a time when they made me go in during the day, I did. Maybe the one thing I did like about being retired was sleeping until the afternoon.

But now it was late, and for Trawler to be calling me meant there was a problem. Six months after the last time I'd carried a sigil and a wand there were only two problems around that warranted a chime just shy of midnight.

There might be a problem with a case I'd worked in the past. Sometimes a poor former-Detective might be invited in to consult, or maybe even head out to a scene just to render some opinions. Every once in a while something useful would crop up as a result, but more often than not it was cop courtesy to make the old stallions feel useful.

Then again, sometimes the problem was with the young stallions. Like my ex-partner—and, arguably, one of my only friends still breathing—Detective Second Class Griffon Dire.

I went with assuming the more likely.

"What's he done?" I asked.

"He hasn't chimed?" The dwarf sounded surprised. Not unreasonable. It was unusual that I hadn't seen or heard from Griff in a couple of weeks.

"It's been a little bit. I figured things had gotten busy."

"Dire has, at least." Trawler sighed. Uncharacteristic of him, but I wasn't one of his officers to cow anymore. I was his expert consultant on—and what passed for the counselor to—one of his primeshift Homicide Unit detectives. That made me a peer in a way our ranks had never worked out to, despite the fact that we'd only joined the department a few years apart.

"Just tell me, Argo. I'd rather know the bad news than guess at it."

"Why don't you come in? I've got a bottle, and he's driving me to it. May as well have company to make me feel less degenerate."

Twist my arm why don't you? "Sure. I'll be right in."

"Thanks. See you," he said, then he'd slammed down the horn on his clarion.

Smiling at the no-bullshit senior officer I knew—and tolerated—I downed the bourbon and went looking for my keys.

I pulled up to the entrance to the parking structure under Hammersmith watchtower and nodded to the uniformed officer guarding the entrance. I raised my retiree's identification card. He raised the boom and waved me through. I didn't recognize him, so I drove by without stopping to greet him

The garage was buzzing as midnight rolled closer. Despite all this activity, the shift change from nightshift to graveshift always brought with it a strangely somber feel. Some of the worst hours of the day had just passed, but the most abysmal were about to begin. Everyone on the Job knew it, so the ticking over to a new day was given ample respect.

My old parking space was empty, so I snuck my new carry into it. I could have—should have, even—slipped the Kandry Raven into one of the visitor spots. After all, there were plenty of them, and almost no visitors this late. But most days I still felt like I'd just gone to sleep and had a dream that I'd done something stupid and retired.

Trawler had asked me if I wanted to come back once. It was about two, or maybe even three months after I retired. But my answer had been simple, and he'd respected it. Even though I wasn't as old as he was, I felt twice his age. I'd probably go to my grave as ready to fight as I'd come into the world, but my time chasing down killers was at an end.

Still, I'd cried afterward. A whole two or three tears had escaped my eyes and rolled down my cheeks after I'd laid down the horn. That fucking dwarf sure knew how to make a guy feel like he was useful.

But even Trawler wouldn't have me come down to the watchtower for no reason. So I made my way to the lift and up to the third floor where he'd taken up residence after inheriting command of Hammersmith.

Most Captains would have taken the spread on the thirteenth floor. Not Argo. He'd made adjustments to the records area and carved himself out an office between HU and RU, his two loves, and what he called the lifeblood of the specialty units. Usually in private of course. Bad for morale to let the Historical Crimes Unit detectives know how useless they are.

So as I headed towards the dwarf's domain I passed my old haunt. None of the homicide detectives —nightshift or graveshift—were in the bull pen, so I wandered back to my desk. It was still empty; which gave me some kind of an idea of how things were going. Primeshift was still down a detective, and it meant that Bird-n-Prey were probably on their own out on the streets, because last I'd heard Griff was still pissed about being sidelined.

Ever since that fucking case. Dire had gone above and beyond. Too far beyond. My oldest friend in the world had been killed, and my partner had made it his mission to make sure we got what we needed to crack the case. He'd done it despite how much shit I'd thrown at him that week. In the end he'd proven he was willing to risk anything for me.

Two months ago we'd sat together in a courtroom, quietly listening to Lannik Mann go down for executing my friend. Gallan Murder—who'd taken the name Armos—had justice because of just how far my partner had gone on our final ride.

Griff had been riding a desk since that day. Because of me. It was the least I could do for him after six years. He needed protection from himself. And besides, it was my fault he'd become an officer. He was my responsibility, all the way.

I pressed my hand into the surface of my former-desk. It was cold. The fucking thing needed a detective sweating over it again. It needed stacks of papers. A cup of coffee. Life.

I sighed and turned away. Maybe three strides later I reversed course, walked back to the pair of desks, and picked up a stylus and piece of paper from my ex-partner's workspace. It took me a minute to scribble the note and drop it in the bottom drawer. He'd find it eventually. Probably when he went for the bottle he kept inside.

My communion accomplished, I made my way out of the bull pen and headed to see Trawler.

☆   ☆   ☆
      ☆   ☆
                ☆

The Captain was sitting in his tall chair behind his massive desk when I entered his office. Papers were everywhere, as usual. Seeing the stacks always made me glad I hadn't advanced any higher.

"Captain," I said.

"Thief. Have a seat," said the dwarf as he poured me a drink. I grabbed one of the pair of chairs he kept for the rare cases when he wasn't chewing someone out and dragged it closer to the bureau. When I was seated we raised our glasses and tilted them to each other.

"Health," I said.

"Fortune," he replied.

The liquid was fine stuff. A cognac from one of the western kingdoms, no doubt. Argo's taste in alcohol is much more refined than the beer and ale so stereotypical of dwarven culture. I may prefer my brandy, but at least the Captain doesn't offer his honored guests vinegar when they make appearances in the middle of the night.

"So," I said, then chased another sip of the amber draught. "So—and by the way, fucking fine stuff, this—"

"Thanks."

"—what's he done now?" I finished asking.

The Captain grimaced. "He really didn't tell you about Dead's Night, did he?"

"I haven't talked to him since before that. What happened?"

"He was out in Black Spit visiting that Army buddy of his—"

"Durrin, from the SOD."

"Yeah. He was visiting Durrin for a party. Just a normal

masquerade. Some drinks, some neighbors. I guess he's a popular guy."

"He does neighborhood service. Works with kids. He grew up in Black Spit, got out, and made himself into something in the Army."

Trawler nodded. "Figures that Dire would have latched onto him."

"I dunno. He latched onto me. Shows a lack of discerning taste."

"You sell yourself too short, Hargold." Argo unstopped the bottle and refilled his glass. I held mine out and he obliged me.

"Black Spit?" Dire and I have a history in that ward. It's where we met.

"Patrol unit called for backup and, of course, all the other units were busy responding to calls."

"So Dire was close."

"Yeah. Suspected stolen vehicle. Real classy carriage, driving around Black Spit."

"They ran it."

"It came back reported stolen. They don't stop anyone alone in that ward. They'd rather have three or four units if they can."

"I'm aware." What I didn't share was that I was of the opinion that Dire was worth three or four units alone.

"You know there's reasons."

"I've worked enough cases in there when I was running graveshift in Social Crimes Division to know it gets bad."

"You remember that story you always tell about the night you met?"

"The night Dire and I met?" I snorted. "Idiot nearly got himself killed taking on five guys who were raping one of my squadmates." I took a sip of the cognac and shrugged. "Brave as fuck though. Damned admirable, you know?"

Argo nodded. "Yes. Brave. Stupid. Heroic. Impulsive."

"All synonyms for Griff." I sighed and chased cognac.

"They came under fire while approaching the vehicle. One of the patrol officers went down in the initial exchange—no, fuck that, ambush—they didn't even get a chance to return fire at first."

I leaned forward, heart hammering. "What?"

"I don't know why he didn't tell you, Hargold."

"What the fuck happened, Argo?"

"The Corporal did her best to return fire while Griff dragged her partner to cover. He called for backup, but they were within an exclusion zone, and all other units were still unavailable."

"So they couldn't get any chirurgeon's wagons in there. The Warrens?"

The dwarf nodded. "They were a couple blocks away. So here's where it gets a little less definite. According to Corporal Stance, Griffon ordered her to carry her partner, Halbern, all the way to the rendezvous point. He relieved the fallen officer of some of his gear, including a service wand, and stayed to cover her."

"So after that only Griffon reported events."

"Not entirely, but for much of it, yeah. Stance says that before she managed to get clear she saw Griff down one assailant. The backup units arrived to find Dire's Hallowstone a flaming wreck, the patrol unit badly damaged from stray blasts, and two masked individuals who had been killed with ice wand blasts consistent with service issue wands. Later on he confirmed that he'd been the one who killed them."

"Wait, they discovered all that at the site of the original stop, but no Griff?"

"He pursued."

"He *what?*"

"He cut his link at the start of the Warrens, but dispatch had him headed in at high speed. *Very* high speed. Like he'd taken a vehicle. Only he was moving down a shopping arcade with barriers in place."

"Shit."

"Care to tell me what kind of shit he got himself into in Heartcore six months ago?"

I remained silent. What Griff can do scares the fuck out of

me. Mostly because I don't think he's got a clue what it all is. Also, what we did the day we took down Mann was illegal, unethical, and could potentially get all of us—Falcon and Rabino included—thrown in prison.

"Fine, Thief. You know I had to ask." The dwarf shook his head. "He's an idiot, like you said. The NDPD has an official hands-off policy where the Warrens are concerned. In the entire time I've been on the Job there's been one other time when we went in, and that was in watchtower contingent strength, plus specialist squads."

"When was that?" I wondered if I'd missed that day.

"I was still on patrol."

"Shit."

"Yeah. That long."

"What happened in there?"

"Details are sketchy."

"He's not sharing." I smoothed my hair back and then fluffed it up again.

The Captain seemed pensive as he nodded and rubbed his neat beard. After a few moments he spoke again. "What we have in the hour afterward is this." He started to tick off fingers. "One, another dead assailant. Griff classified him as 'killed by a errant blast' during a showdown in one of the tower blocks."

"Can happen." I said.

"He took a single ice wand blast through the throat from range longer than short and DMU says no way Griffon could have discharged the wand given the disposition of the other casualties."

"Huh. That's a damned lucky accidental hit."

"Two, a hamstrung dwarf which we know was taken down by Dire's knife."

"He only pulls that when he's got nothing else."

The dwarf nodded. "Then we have three, a man shot in the shoulder—again not something DMU says Griff could have managed—"

"He did *not* have a wand if he had his knife out."

"I agree, and DMU is positive, but Griff swears these wounds were simply accidents of combat and that they came from another assailant who fled. Damage done to Dire's vest makes it hard to tell what happened at what point during his evening. But they can say he was surely struck by blasts from just about every angle."

"None of that makes any kind of sense." *Unless he's covering for someone,* I didn't say.

"Anyway, the man with the shoulder wound was fairly superficially wounded and subsequently engaged in close quarters combat with Griff."

"I bet he wasn't superficially wounded after making that mistake." I'm physically intimidating, but Griffon's hand-to-hand skills are terrifying. He's the only other cop I've ever met, outside of maybe Trawler, who I'd be worried about taking on.

"Actually, Griffon got it pretty bad. Three cracked ribs, a broken nose, and bruises everywhere. Not to mention the fact that he was shot in the leg twice at some point."

"Same leg?"

"Yeah, the left. But you're right. The grappling ended with Griff snapping the man's forearm cleanly in half."

I cringed. "Fuck."

"The other casualty on the scene was a middle-aged gnome who took a stray blast from the same weapon which nearly killed the patrol officer. Both the gnome and the officer survived."

"So Griff killed two suspects, pursued four more into the Warrens, killed another, subdued two, and let one escape?"

"Yes."

"I can see your problem."

"Good, bec—"

"You're trying to figure out how to make copies of him."

"Ha. Yes, Thief. I need more rogue homicide detectives."

"Unorthodox," I said with a slight smile, "but scarily effective."

Trawler didn't buy it. He was a good Captain. "You're afraid for him too."

I took a moment, but eventually I nodded. "I am."

The dwarf reached into his desk and pulled out a stack of folders. "This is it. This is his last chance." He patted the files. "If this doesn't work I have to cut him loose. He's too dangerous when unchecked."

"Is that why you asked me to come back?"

"Yes, and no." He smiled at me. "Honestly, you're one of the best homicide cops I've ever met, and Dire is as good as he is because of you. You're an asset, even though you think you're too old. But yeah, I need him under control."

I started to reach for the files and paused. "Wait a minute, Argo. You said he'd gotten in trouble twice."

"Today he nearly got his head blown off by a fire rod."

"I thought he was still riding a desk."

"I had to put him back on active duty. Central demanded it after what he did saving that officer. Halbern. His partner, Corporal Stance, has been very busy singing your partner's praises to anyone and everyone who'll listen. And honestly, she has a point."

"But he almost got killed immediately after you put him on the streets."

Trawler shrugged. "True. But the worst of it is he lost that damned hat. Poof. Ashes."

"No."

"I can't believe he didn't chime you to arrange a funeral for the fucking thing."

We laughed for a minute at that. The cognac was definitely having an effect on us both. He refilled our drinks and we moved back to the point.

"If I can't get him to accept a partner he's got to go." He pushed the folders across the bureau. "These are his options."

"What am I supposed to do?" I asked as I took the files.

"Pick your successor."

"They're going to be assigned to homicide?"

"Not all of them, no. Fartower—"

I laughed. "No."

"Ahem. Fartower would mean he'd be transferred to HCU."

"Not happening."

"Most of the rest would mean Griff stays on HU's primeshift. There's an OCU slot there with a pretty good D1c. Mostly other second classes. A third who lost his partner and needs a new mentor..." He trailed off, holding something back.

"What?"

"Just another problem child. I don't really want to compound my issues."

I started flipping through the files. He let me read in silence for a while.

After I finished the stack I dropped them in two piles I'd mentally declared 'no fucking way' and 'are you kidding me' and sighed. "I really hate to ask, but I didn't see his file in those...so where's the other problem child's folder?"

"None of the others?" He looked as if I'd just confirmed his worst fears.

"They'll never be able to keep his interest or keep him in check. Fartower is the best detective you have in there, but Dire will quit on his own if you assign him to HCU. And let's be honest, Argo. That squad needs Fartower to close even as few cases as they manage every year."

He slid the drawer open again and tossed me a single file. "I can't figure out what to do with this one. I've only known about her for a week, and it just seems wrong to sink Dire like that. He deserves a shot at making it. The department needs cops like him."

I tilted my head. He shrugged and waved a stubby-fingered hand at the file. I picked it up and started to leaf through it.

It took me about two seconds to spot the problem. "You cannot be serious."

He shook his head. "It's real. She graduates next week. She's close to top of her class, too."

After a few moments I realized that my jaw had fallen open, so I forced my mouth closed again. "You know what?" I tapped the file and smiled down at the pretty young blonde's picture.

"Mmm?"

"He won't know what hit him. She's fucking perfect."

I tossed the folder back on the desk and raised my glass. Trawler lifted his as well. "If you're sure?"

I nodded. "To partners."

"Old and new," said Argo.

"Old and new," I agreed.

AFTERWORD

What is there to say after finishing the first collection? Outside of "phew" or "wahoo" I just don't know how to express it.

The series arc was always intended to illustrate a few things. I'm hoping I managed at least part of what I set out to do with the words, of course, but mostly I hope to have entertained you. I chose this particular project to make my first self-published effort because the concept appealed to me, and it's been done so seldom that I wanted to read it. If someone else wasn't going to give me a police procedural with magic and strange beings, I'd just need to do it myself.

So I'm enjoying getting into the universe myself. And maybe not so much enjoying, but at least feeling accomplished as I navigate the related world of publishing. It's not easy to have to deal with everything, and I can certainly see why one might just hand everything but the writing off to someone else to handle. Yet I've always been someone who likes to do things in my own way, and this is how I can as a writer.

If you're eager for more, the series is being made available at intervals of about two weeks electronically, which means that the print versions come out about every eight weeks. The next series is *The Uniform*, and the stories will be covering a different officer, starting with Trawler and Thief in the first volume, *Radical Plot*. (Which is actually Thief's tale. Trawler's story leads the volume off, and is called *Lightning Riot*.) So the print compilation of *The Uniform* will be out by May.

Also to look forward to: the first novel will be out in the not-too-distant future. I just don't have a hard date for it. But rest assured, the *Dire Crimes* series itself will be kicking off within the first half of the year.

I said it once in the dedication, and I'll say it one more time here. My son, Ethan, fell ill and passed away in 2009. He was two. It is in large part due to him that I had started pushing to write in the time before he passed. His life—and my eternal love for him—certainly still plays a major role in what drives me to create. I miss him. This volume, my first full-length work, could only have ever been for him.

But thanks are in order for the living as well. Megan catches my mistakes when I'm too tired to tell an "is" from an "it" and the book which you've just finished would be much less polished were she not so diligent. Bridgette gets kudos for many things, but as usual it's worth thanking her for the cover, which is the design we worked up in conjunction with the community on KBoards.com. If you love it, it's all her and the folks who made suggestions. If you hate it, blame me for being a control-hungry artist. Fair enough?

J.C., Christine, Shabnam, Richard, and Adam all get thanks for various things. My children, Ash and Dec, are to be commended for their swiftly developing ability to whine in concert. The dog—and her piteous eyes—must never be forgotten.

But so very, very important, and never forgotten: you, the reader. Thank you. I hope you've enjoyed reading, and I hope you'll be back for more. Because there's a lot coming up in the *Dire Crimes* universe!

Mathew Reuther
March 9, 2013
Vista, CA

ABOUT THE AUTHOR

Mathew is bi-lingual, holds dual-citizenship, and has a pair of hands. This last part is particularly convenient because typing with only five digits is pretty slow going.

As a native Seattleite (and subsequent 8-year resident of the Netherlands), Mathew is no stranger to rain. But since 2009 he's lived in the San Diego area, and basked in the shine of the Southern Californian sun.

Mathew's education in the arts started early. As the child of two artists (a musician and an actor) who just happen to be teachers, it was perhaps his destiny to become a wordsmith.

Legend holds that as a wee babe Mathew was passed around the dim backstage of a theatre during production after production. It was during this time that the drama and storytelling floating in the atmosphere seeped into the very fiber of his being.

With two kids, a dumb dog, and a fantastic wife, Mathew is presently living the dream he's harbored deep inside for most of his life: to raise a family and write at least fifty damn novels. Keep following him to see how that all works out.

Mailing list (case sensitive): eepurl.com/skNdr

Website: mathewreuther.com
Twitter: twitter.com/mathew_reuther
Facebook: facebook.com/mathewreuther0
Goodreads: goodreads.com/mathew_reuther

ABOUT DIRE CALLS

Murder in the big city. Tall, dark, and handsome detective. A cast of extras from the grizzled veteran to the flirtatious crime scene crush.

Think you've heard this one before?

Think again.

We're not talking about some hackneyed Chi-town cop, and this sprawling metropolis isn't the kind of melting pot you're used to. Step out onto these mean streets and you've got bigger problems to deal with than Catholic dogma, Latin Kings machismo, or Teamster muscle.

Detective Griffon Dire works the Hammersmith watchtower in the City-State of New Dagonia. Officers on the Job for the NDPD don't wave a gun and a badge; they're strapped with a fully-charged wand and flash a sigil when they kick in a door. You want to talk about a rough day at the office? Dire is up against the likes of the fanatical Spearsworn, the cutthroat Goblin Court, and the intractable Lorry League. *And that's just Tuesday.*

So, no, this *isn't* your grandmother's crime novel.

Dire Calls shorts are fast, smart, and modern. They're fantasy for thriller buffs; mystery for magic lovers. The series pays homage to the grand tradition of cop fiction while blazing a bold new trail of its own.

The *Dire Crimes* series will change the way you look at police procedurals forever.

visit **DIRE CRIMES**.COM